OUTLAW RANGER: VOLUME ONE

JAMES REASONER

WOLFPACK
PUBLISHING
— EST 2013 —

Outlaw Ranger, Volume One
Print Edition
© Copyright 2021 (As Revised) James Reasoner

Wolfpack Publishing
5130 S. Fort Apache Rd. 215-380
Las Vegas, NV 89148

wolfpackpublishing.com

eBook ISBN 978-1-64734-765-9
Paperback ISBN 978-1-63977-026-7

OUTLAW RANGER: VOLUME ONE

OUTLAW RANGER

SOUTH TEXAS, 1900

DEMONS ROAMED THE CHAPARRAL.

Not the sort that came from Hell, of course, although some might say this South Texas brush country bore a distinct resemblance to Hades, especially in the summer. It was hot as hell today, G.W. Braddock thought as he knelt with a Winchester in his hands and listened intently. He was a lean, sandy-haired man with a thick mustache of the same shade. A cloudless, brassy blue sky arched above him.

Somewhere out there in that brasada were Tull Coleman and his gang. Braddock had trailed them north from Corpus Christi where they had held up a bank and gunned down a young teller foolish enough to try to tackle one of Coleman's men. Then, as if for good measure, they had ridden down a young woman during their getaway, trampling and breaking her under their horses' hooves, leaving behind a grief-stricken husband and an 18-month-old daughter without a mama.

Braddock wished he could kill every one of the sons of bitches.

That wasn't his job, though. The star-in-a-circle Texas Ranger badge pinned to his faded blue shirt meant he just took them in. It was the responsibility of a judge and jury to mete out justice.

Of course, if he had to put bullets through a few of them in the process of making that arrest, it wasn't going to break his heart. There was also the little matter of self-defense. They wanted to kill him as much as he wanted to kill them—they had already shot his horse out from under him—and he had a right to try to stop them.

So come on, Tull, he thought. *Where the hell are you?*

A faint crackling sound drifted through the hot, still air. Something was moving in the brush to Braddock's right. It might be a javelina, he told himself...or it might be an owlhoot bent on shooting a Texas Ranger. Slowly, Braddock swiveled toward the sound and lifted the Winchester. His finger curled around the trigger.

One of the wild pigs that roamed this area burst out of the chaparral and lunged at Braddock, squealing. He didn't want to shoot and give away his position unless he had to, so he flung himself aside. The javelina rammed his left shoulder and he felt the animal's tusks tear through his shirt and scrape his hide. He was already a little off-balance, and the impact of the collision knocked him to the ground.

Several men charged out of the brush and whooped with excitement. One of them, a chunky hombre with a square head and black beard, kicked the Winchester out of Braddock's hands. Another tried to stomp his chest and cave in his ribs. Braddock caught hold of the man's boot just in time to save himself from that. He heaved on the outlaw's leg and toppled him over backward.

The fallen man got tangled up with the other two and that gave Braddock time to roll away from them and get up on his knees. He reached for the Colt on his hip, experiencing as he did so a split-second's worry that the gun might have fallen out of its holster while he was thrashing around on the ground.

Then his hand closed around the walnut grips and he felt the immense comfort of knowing that he was still armed. He pulled the Colt and shot the big, black-bearded man in the chest. The man rocked back a step as his eyes widened in surprise and then bugged out even more in pain. He felt of his chest where blood was welling out of the bullet hole as if to convince himself that he really was wounded.

Then he pitched forward on his face.

Before the bearded man hit the ground, Braddock had shifted the Colt and fired again, this time at a man with a fox-like face under a straw Stetson with a tightly curled brim that drooped down in front. Braddock's bullet struck him in his weak chin and angled up through his brain before blowing out the back of his skull. He dropped straight down, already dead.

That left the man who had tried to stomp Braddock. He scrambled onto hands and knees and then lunged to his feet and turned his back on the Ranger as he tried to flee. Clearly, all the fight had gone out of him now that his two companions were dead.

Braddock aimed this time instead of letting luck and instinct guide his shot. The third outlaw stumbled in his flight as Braddock's slug struck him in the small of his back and broke his spine. He tumbled to the ground and lay there screaming until he passed out about ten seconds later.

Braddock sat there breathing a little hard as he looked at the bodies scattered around him. He knew good fortune had been with him. Most men didn't survive three-to-one odds.

Unfortunately, there was a good chance three more outlaws still lurked out there in the thick brush...and one of them was Tull Coleman.

With the efficiency born of long practice, Braddock broke open the Colt and shook out the three empties, then thumbed fresh cartridges into the cylinder. He snapped it closed and pouched the iron. On hands and knees, he crawled over to where his Winchester had landed. He picked it up and made sure the sandy ground hadn't fouled the barrel.

Fully armed again, Braddock resumed sitting and waiting. His pulse had slowed down a little now. A few minutes earlier, in the aftermath of the fight, it had been pounding fit to beat the band.

Every instinct in his body told him that Tull Coleman had been close enough to hear the three shots, followed briefly by the wounded man's screams. Coleman would be too curious to just let that go. He would have to come see what had happened.

The man with the bullet in his back groaned as he regained consciousness. When he fell, he had landed facing away from Braddock. Now he said, "Ranger...Ranger, are you there? I can't see you."

Braddock didn't reply. He didn't have anything to say to the outlaw right now.

"Ranger, I...I'm hurt mighty bad. I think my back's broke. I need help. You got to get me to a doctor."

That poor woman down in Corpus Christi had had her back broken, too, along with plenty of other bones, when Coleman's gang stampeded over her. They could have swerved around her but, according to the witnesses Braddock had talked to, it had looked like Tull Coleman, who was in the lead, had ridden toward her on purpose. It was hard to believe that anybody could be that lowdown.

Braddock could believe it of Coleman, though. The outlaw had a reputation for violence and brutality as did those who rode with him.

"Ranger? Ranger?...Oh, Lord, he shot me down and left me here to die. That star-packin' bastard." The wounded outlaw sobbed a couple of times, then raised his voice and called, "Tull! Tull, he ain't here no more! He shot me in the back and run off! I need help, Tull. I'm hurt bad."

The brasada was quiet. Even the little animals were silent, gone to ground because of the shots. The javelina that had knocked Braddock on his butt was long gone. The tusker hadn't even slowed down. Braddock was convinced that the three outlaws had spooked the animal and sent it charging through the brush in an attempt to flush him out.

That idea had backfired on them.

"Tull? I...I think Franklin and Tillotson are both dead. That damn Ranger bushwhacked us! We never had a chance."

Well, that was one way of explaining how come he'd been shot in the back, Braddock thought with a faint smile.

"Please..." The man's voice was weakening. He'd lost

a considerable amount of blood and might well be on the verge of passing out. "Tull..."

Somebody or something moved in the brush.

The noises came closer. Braddock took advantage of them and retreated farther into the chaparral. The crackling covered any sounds his own movements caused. He stopped when there was a nice screen of mesquite branches between him and the wounded man.

A figure stepped out of the brush and bent over the fallen outlaw. He was short and stocky, a Mexican with his sombrero hanging behind his neck by its chin strap. Not Tull Coleman. Raul Gomez, Braddock decided. Gomez was on record as being one of Coleman's bunch.

"Jeff, you gone and got yourself killed," Gomez said.

"No, no, I'll be all right," the wounded man babbled. "I...I just need a sawbones."

"I don't think so. I seen men shot like that before. Even if you don't die, you won't never walk again, *amigo*. Better to go ahead and put you out of your misery right here and now."

Gomez shucked his Colt from leather and pointed it at the back of Jeff's head, clearly intending to blow his fellow outlaw's brains out. Braddock knew he ought to let Gomez go ahead and pull the trigger but, instead, he stepped out of the brush, leveled his rifle, and said, "Hold it, Gomez."

The Mexican was turned half away from him. Gomez tried to twist around and bring up the revolver. Braddock squeezed the Winchester's trigger and sent a .44-40 round ripping through Gomez's lungs. The outlaw's Colt boomed as his finger contracted on the trigger but the bullet tore harmlessly through the brush. The shot spun Gomez off his feet. He lay on the ground struggling to drag rasping, bubbling breaths into his body as he drowned in his own blood.

With a crash of brush, another man appeared to Braddock's left. He had a gun in each hand and fired both of them as fast as he could thumb the hammers back. He sprayed a lot of lead around but, rushing his shots like that, he failed to hit the Ranger with any of them. Braddock loosed another round from the Winchester, levered the rifle, fired again. Both shots punched into the outlaw's chest at close range. They lifted him off his feet and threw him backward.

With his ears ringing from all those shots, Braddock couldn't hear much of anything. So it wasn't a noise that warned him but rather instinct. He sensed someone coming at him from behind and tried to turn.

That movement was enough to cause the knife to merely rip a gash along his left collarbone instead of plunging into his back and skewering his heart. It still hurt like blazes and the pain drew a yell from Braddock's throat. He struck upward with the rifle butt and dug it under Tull Coleman's jaw. Coleman grunted but continued bulling against Braddock. The Ranger couldn't stay on his feet. Both men went down.

Coleman was wiry and fought like a wildcat. He slashed at Braddock with the Bowie knife in his hand. According to the reports the Rangers had, the heavy blade was Coleman's favorite weapon and he was good with it. Braddock had all he could do to block the knife with the Winchester's barrel, steel ringing against steel as he did so. The rifle's length made it awkward to handle in these close quarters, though, and Braddock knew it was only a matter of time before Coleman slipped past his guard and buried the Bowie in his guts.

Braddock let go of the Winchester with his right hand and shot that fist forward in a short but powerful blow that landed squarely on Coleman's nose. He felt cartilage crunch and flatten under the impact. Blood squirted hotly across his knuckles. Coleman's head rocked back from the force of the punch and Braddock hit him again before he could recover.

While Coleman was half-stunned, Braddock cracked the rifle barrel against his wrist. That made Coleman drop the knife. Braddock lifted the Winchester and brought the butt down into Coleman's face, doing even more damage to the outlaw's bloody, battered features. Coleman went limp. He was either unconscious or dead, and at the moment, Braddock didn't give a damn which.

Braddock planted the rifle butt against the ground and used it to help lever himself to his feet. With his chest heaving from all the exertion, he looked around at the six outlaws. Four of them were dead, he was pretty sure of that. Jeff was still alive. Braddock could hear his strained breathing. Coleman's chest rose and fell raggedly so he was alive, too.

This had been a hell of a fight, Braddock thought. Six against one and he was still alive and relatively unharmed. The gash on his back from Coleman's Bowie burned like fire but Braddock didn't figure it was serious. If he was the sort to brag or be full of himself, he would say this was a legendary battle, the kind of fracas that folks would talk about for a long time to come.

But he didn't care about anything like that, only

about bringing these killers and thieves to justice. That was his job and he did it as well as he could.

However, he did allow himself one moment, as he was reloading the Winchester, to smile grimly to himself and say in a quiet voice, "How about that, Pa? That good enough for you?"

2

TWO DAYS LATER, BRADDOCK DROVE A WAGON INTO SAN Antonio. He had commandeered it from a farm at the edge of the chaparral with a promise that it would be returned. Jeff Hawley, the outlaw he'd shot in the back, was still alive somehow and lay face down on a pallet of blankets in the wagon bed. Braddock had patched him up as best he could. Hawley was in and out of consciousness, incoherent much of the time when he was awake and cursing bitterly the rest of the time.

Tull Coleman was in the wagon bed, too, wearing shackles and leg irons. He didn't waste his breath cussing. Anyway, his jaw was still swollen from Braddock clouting him with the rifle butt, so it probably hurt to talk.

Braddock had left the bodies of the four dead outlaws with the marshal in the nearest town. The lawman had promised he would see to it that the men were buried, although the State of Texas would have to foot the bill, he'd warned. Couldn't ask the local undertaker to work for free. Braddock had agreed to that although he didn't know if the request would be honored. All he knew was that he wanted the corpses off his hands. They would have stunk to high heaven if he'd had to take them all the way to San Antonio.

Braddock brought the team to a halt in front of the adobe building in Military Plaza that housed the headquarters of Company D. A couple of Rangers lounged near the entrance, puffing on quirlies and joshing with each other. They straightened and looked with interest into the back of the wagon.

"What you got there, Junior?" one of them asked.

Braddock's jaw tightened. He hated to be called Junior. Hadn't liked it when he was a kid, didn't like it even more now. But there was no denying that a lot of his fellow Rangers thought of him that way. It was unavoidable when he had the same name as his father.

The elder Braddock had been a sergeant in the Frontier Battalion under Major John B. Jones, the battalion's first commander. Sergeant George Washington Braddock Sr. had made a fine name for himself twenty-five years earlier, fighting outlaws and hostile Indians from San Antonio to El Paso. That was quite a legacy to live up to.

"Good Lord," the second Ranger exclaimed. "That's Tull Coleman, big as life."

"And twice as ugly," the first Ranger agreed. He let out a whistle of admiration. "Looks like you did a good job, Braddock. Lawmen have been lookin' for this varmint all over South Texas."

Braddock set the brake and climbed down from the wagon seat. His movements were stiff and awkward because his back still hurt where Coleman had cut him. He had started to wonder if the wound had festered.

"Captain Hughes inside?" he asked. When the two Rangers nodded, he went on, "Reckon you could see to locking up these boys? You'll have to take the wounded one over to Doc Sullivan's house and put a guard over him."

"Sure," one of the men said. "Say, Junior, have you heard the news?"

"News?" Braddock frowned. "What news?"

The other man nudged his companion and shook his head.

"You just go on in and report to the captain, Braddock. If he wants to tell you anything, he will."

Braddock didn't like the sound of that. Something was wrong and he figured the quickest way to find out what it was would be to go inside and talk to the captain. He pointed to Coleman and told the other Rangers, "Keep a close eye on him. He's a tricky son of a bitch."

Braddock's boot heels rang on the polished wooden floor as a clerk showed him to Captain Hughes' office. Normally, the thick adobe walls meant it was cooler inside the headquarters building than out but that didn't seem to be the case today. The air was hot and stifling and Braddock had trouble getting his breath.

Captain John R. Hughes was built solid as a rock. His face was broad and sported a neat mustache. His brown hair was parted in the middle. When Braddock came in, Hughes stood up and reached across the desk to shake his hand.

"Private Braddock," Hughes said. "I got a telegram

informing me that you were bringing in Tull Coleman and one member of his gang."

Hughes didn't ask him to sit, so Braddock remained standing. He nodded and said, "That's right, Captain. The other fella is Jeff Hawley. He's wounded but he seems bound and determined not to die. Stubborn critter."

"What about the others who robbed that bank in Corpus?"

"They didn't want to come along peacefully," Braddock said, not offering any other explanation.

Hughes nodded slowly. "I see," he said. "That'll all be in your report?"

"Sure," Braddock replied with a shrug. He didn't care for writing reports but he supposed it was just part of the job.

"That's good. Turn it in to me as soon as you're done." Hughes paused, drew in a deep breath, and went on with obvious reluctance, "I'm sorry to say that'll be your last official act as a Ranger, Private."

Braddock thought the air in here had gotten even hotter and it made him so uncomfortable that for a moment he didn't comprehend what Hughes had just said. When the captain's meaning finally sunk in on his brain, he stared at Hughes and said, "You're kicking me out of the Rangers? What the hell for?"

Hughes' features tightened. Braddock knew the captain didn't like profanity and his tone had been disrespectful, to boot. He felt too bad and was too angry to care. Hughes said, "This isn't my idea, Braddock. The Rangers are being disbanded."

That news was so shocking it made Braddock dizzy. He put a hand on the back of the chair in front of the desk to steady himself as he said, "That's loco, Captain. Why would Texas get rid of the Rangers?"

With his mouth twisting as if he had just bitten into a rotten apple, Hughes said, "It's not really the state's doing, either. It's all because of the lawyers."

Braddock shook his head and wished he hadn't because the motion just made him dizzier. "I don't understand."

"Some lawyer found something in the legislation that created the Rangers, back in 1874, that says only officers have the power to make legal arrests."

"I'm an officer," Braddock insisted. "An officer of the law."

"You're a private in the Texas Rangers. According to the letter of the law, you don't have the legal authority to do much of anything."

"I just brought in Tull Coleman and Jeff Hawley!"

Hughes sighed, shook his head, and said, "They'll probably have to be released. All the prisoners the Rangers have brought in who haven't already been tried and convicted are being let go. There are a dozen motions in the court to have those prior convictions vacated as well but all that is still up in the air. For now, all that really matters is that the Rangers are finished."

"No!" Braddock had to lean heavier on the chair to hold himself up. "No. My pa devoted his whole life to the Rangers. He raised me to be a Ranger. They can't be done away with because of some...some piss-ant lawyer!"

"I'm sorry, Braddock. It's out of my hands." Hughes paused. "Braddock? Are you all right? You look a little —Braddock!"

The captain's startled voice was the last thing Braddock heard. His head was spinning so bad it seemed like it was about to fly off his shoulders. He tried to brace himself on the chair but his fingers slid off. The floor jumped up and slammed him in the face.

That was the last thing Braddock knew for what seemed like a very long time.

———

"WHAT THE HELL ARE YOU DOIN', cryin' over a damn dog?"

"He was my friend," George said as he patted down the dirt mounded on the grave he had dug himself. He tried not to sniffle. He knew his father hated crying, especially in men. Of course, at eight years old, he wasn't exactly a man but Pa wouldn't care about that. He'd still fetch George a clout on the head if he got annoyed enough.

"He was a dumb animal. Couldn't be a friend to you nor nobody else. Jus' a dumb animal."

George didn't say anything. Arguing with his father really was pointless.

Pa kicked at the grave. "Get up and get on about your chores. The comp'ny's ridin' out tomorrow to hunt down some Mex bandidos. You'll have to keep the place goin' while I'm gone, same as usual. You know your ma's too sickly to do much." Under his breath, he added, "And you ain't much better, boy."

George pretended not to hear. He got to his feet and turned to head for the barn. His father was right. There were chores to be done. He had to be dependable. Rangers were dependable and he was going to grow up to be a Ranger. That was just the way of things.

But he couldn't stop himself from glancing back at the spot where he had laid his dog to rest. He started to mouth a farewell and that was when he sensed his father's big hand coming at his head. George ducked the slap and broke into a stumbling run toward the barn.

"Get along with you!" the sergeant called after him. "Get along, you worthless little piss-ant! Good Lord, how'm I ever gonna make a Ranger out of a sorry specimen like you?"

3

It was like being trapped in a mudhole with the thick, slimy stuff trying to drag him under and clog his mouth and nose and drown him. Braddock fought desperately, clawing at the muck as it threatened to overwhelm him and, when he finally broke through the surface and gasped, he realized he wasn't drowning at all.

Instead, he was lying in an airy room with big windows and cream-colored walls. The sheets underneath him were wet and uncomfortable. He lifted a trembling hand to his face and found that he was covered with beads of oily sweat.

Something moved to his right. From the corner of his eye, he saw a ghostly, white-clad figure drift into view. A middle-aged woman with a severe face leaned over him and said, "You're awake."

That seemed painfully obvious to Braddock. He opened his mouth and tried to speak but his lips and tongue were too thick and clumsy to form words.

"I'll fetch Dr. Sullivan," the woman said as she retreated from the bedside.

That told Braddock where he was, anyway, and the knowledge was a bit of a relief. He closed his eyes and concentrated on his breathing, which was a little erratic. As it settled into a steadier rhythm, he fought to stay awake. He didn't want to slip back into the hellish world where he had been.

The world of his own past.

A footstep made Braddock open his eyes again. A man with a close-cropped, salt-and-pepper beard had come into the room. Braddock recognized him. Dr. Alfred Sullivan said, "The nurse told me you were awake, Ranger Braddock."

Since he still couldn't talk, Braddock just shook his head.

Sullivan frowned in apparent confusion for a second, then understanding appeared on his face. "Now I know what you mean," he said. "That ridiculous business about the Rangers being disbanded." He reached for something on the bedside table. "Let's get you a drink."

He held a glass to Braddock's lips. Braddock had trouble swallowing but he managed to get some of the water down his throat. He spilled some, too, but that didn't really matter since he was already soaking wet.

He was able to get a few words out after the drink. "Wha...what happened...to me?"

"Blood poisoning from that knife wound in your back, I'd say," Sullivan replied. "You're lucky to be alive. You ran a very high fever for several days. But it's broken now. That's why you're sweating so much. I think you're going to be all right. You'll have to take it easy for a while because you're so weak but with rest and good food you'll recover."

Braddock sighed and let his head sag back against the damp pillow. What was the point of getting better if he couldn't be a Ranger anymore?

From idle curiosity more than anything else, he asked, "How long...was I out?"

"It's been five days since you collapsed in Captain Hughes' office."

Five days, Braddock thought. Almost a week. Lord knew what had happened in that time.

Sullivan gave him another drink, then said, "I'll get Nurse Williams in here to clean you up and change the sheets on the bed and then we need to see if you can take a little broth. You need to start getting your strength back as soon as possible."

Braddock didn't argue but he didn't see why that mattered.

If he couldn't be a Ranger anymore, then nothing mattered.

———

CAPTAIN HUGHES CAME to see Braddock the next day. In a hearty voice, he said, "I thought you'd up and died on me when you collapsed in my office that day, G.W."

Might have been better if he had, Braddock thought. He felt better and was stronger already as his iron constitution asserted itself but he was in no mood for small talk. He said, "What happened to Coleman and Hawley?"

"They're still in custody. I arrested them myself before they could be released."

Braddock was glad to hear that.

Hughes paused, then went on, "I'm not sure how long we'll be able to hold them, though. A lawyer showed up and filed a motion saying they should be released since their original arrest was illegal."

Braddock was sitting up in bed, the wound on his back heavily padded with bandages. Anger stiffened him as he said, "Where in blazes are all these lawyers coming from? They're like cockroaches coming out of a hole!"

"You're not far wrong there," Hughes agreed. He pulled a ladderback chair closer to the bed and sat down. "The Rangers have made a lot of political enemies over the years and some of them have plenty of money to hire lawyers to make things as difficult for us as possible. That's what's going on now. The governor's fighting back, though. I hear that instead of disbanding the Rangers, he's going to issue an order reorganizing the force. The Rangers will still exist but our numbers will be cut drastically. Four companies of six men each is the rumor I'm hearing."

"Twenty-four men to protect the whole state of Texas!"

Hughes shrugged. "Most people don't think the state needs that much protecting anymore. There hasn't been any Indian trouble in years, the border is pretty quiet right now, and most of what we do is chasing down outlaws. People say the county sheriffs and town marshals can handle that just as well. The Frontier Battalion has been too good at its job, G.W. Folks say we're just not needed anymore."

Braddock shook his head and scowled. He said, "They'll be singing a different song when it's their cattle that's been rustled or their loved ones who get gunned down by outlaws."

"You're probably right but, for now, I'll be satisfied just to keep the Rangers in existence, no matter what form it's in. The legislature can write a new law to fix the problem in the old one and then the Rangers can expand again."

One question in particular was nagging at Braddock, so he figured he might as well go ahead and ask it. "Captain...are you going to be able to keep me on as one of those twenty-four men?"

Hughes grimaced and then shook his head. "I wish I could, G.W. You've done a fine job. Your father would have been proud of you."

Braddock doubted that, doubted it very seriously.

"But the few spots we'll have will go to the Rangers who've been on the force the longest, in most cases," the captain went on. "If any of them don't want to keep their jobs, then we'll move on to the next man on the list. You've only been on Company D's rolls for a couple of years, though. I don't see how there would ever be a place for you...at least, not until the legislature passes that new law I mentioned, and the force expands again. Then, maybe..."

"When will that be?"

"To be honest, there's no way of knowing. Like I said, the Rangers have political enemies and they're more dangerous than outlaws. They'll try to block anything that might help us get back to normal."

"It's wrong," Braddock said. "It's all wrong."

"I agree with you but there's nothing we can do except wait to see how the hand plays out."

Weariness washed over Braddock. He was too tired to fight, too worn out to even talk about it anymore. He leaned back against the pillows propped behind him and said, "There's something over there on the dresser you need to take with you, Captain."

"What's that?" Hughes asked as he stood up. He looked down at the dresser, then back over at Braddock with a frown. "You're not talking about your badge, are you?"

"You said I wasn't a Ranger anymore. I don't need it, do I?"

Hughes picked up the star-in-a-circle badge and turned it over in his fingers. "You carved this yourself out of a Mexican peso, didn't you?"

"Yeah. That's what most of the fellas have done."

"Then it's yours. You need to keep it."

Hughes tossed the badge toward Braddock. Out of instinct, Braddock's right hand came up and caught it, plucking the badge deftly from the air. He wouldn't have thought he could react that quickly. He supposed his reflexes were coming back to him.

Hughes picked up his hat. "Don't worry about your medical expenses," he said. "Your injury happened in the line of duty, while you were still working for the State of Texas, so the state will pay for everything."

"Thanks," Braddock said. He couldn't keep a note of bitterness from creeping into his voice.

"I'll be in touch."

Braddock could tell that Hughes wanted to get out of there. He couldn't blame the captain for feeling that way. He just nodded without saying anything and Hughes sighed and went out.

Braddock looked down at the badge lying on his palm. He stared at it for a long time and thought it was funny how a man's whole life could be shaped into a star and trapped inside a silver circle.

THE NEXT DAY, Braddock had a visit from a different lawman. The nurse brought a Bexar County deputy sheriff into the room. She looked uncomfortable and so did the deputy. The nurse got out as quickly as she could.

"How are you doin', Ranger?" the deputy asked.

"A little stronger every day," Braddock replied honestly. He felt like he would be almost back to normal in another week or so. He went on, "But I'm not a Ranger anymore. I reckon you probably know that."

"Yeah. That's, uh, sort of why I'm here." The deputy took a deep breath. "Mr. Braddock, I've got a warrant for your arrest. You'll be under guard here at the doctor's house until he says you're well enough to be moved."

Braddock felt like he'd been punched in the guts. Struggling to control himself, he said, "What are the charges on that warrant?"

"Murder, attempted murder, false arrest, and unlawful imprisonment."

"Who filed those charges?"

"I'm not sure I ought to answer that..."

Braddock said, "By God—", pushed the sheet back and started to swing his legs out of bed.

The deputy held up a hand, palm out, to stop him. "It was a lawyer representin' Tull Coleman and Jeff Hawley. They say you ambushed them and killed four of their friends."

"They were outlaws! They robbed a bank in Corpus Christi and killed two people!"

"They're suspected of it but no charges have been

filed against them yet in Nueces County. That lawyer fella convinced the judge he had to let 'em go since they'd been arrested illegally by, uh, you. And then he turned around and filed the charges against you. The sheriff says we've got to arrest you and let the whole thing run its course."

Braddock sat there stunned. It seemed as if everything in the world had gone wrong suddenly that the way things were supposed to be had been turned on its head.

The deputy thumbed back his hat and went on, "I'll stay here with you until somebody relieves me. Hope you won't hold this against me."

Somehow, Braddock managed to shake his head and say, "You're just doing your job."

The deputy turned the chair around and straddled it. "Yeah, that's the way I'm tryin' to look at it, too, but I got to tell you, it's hard. I mean, hell, you're a Texas Ranger. That's what I wanted to be someday."

Thinking about what Captain Hughes had told him the day before, Braddock said, "It looks like we're both out of luck."

4

THE CASE AGAINST BRADDOCK WAS HEARD BY THE
grand jury a week later. That was pretty fast, due to a
combination of circumstances. The grand jury
happened to be in session and Captain Hughes called
in favors and used his influence to get Braddock's case
moved up on the docket.

Braddock used a cane when he entered the courtroom, but he didn't really need it. The wound on his
back had healed, the blood poisoning was gone, and
most of his strength had returned to him. He wore a
brown tweed suit he had bought for this hearing, all
his other clothes being range garb. His shaggy hair was
trimmed and so was his mustache. His lawyer, a man
named Dunaway whose fee was being paid by Captain
Hughes personally, told Braddock that he looked
properly respectful and respectable for court.

Grand jury proceedings were closed to the public,
so the benches where spectators normally sat were
empty. Braddock and Dunaway sat at one table in the
front of the room while the district attorney sat at the

other, along with Tull Coleman, Jeff Hawley, and their lawyer. Hawley was thin and pale and sat in a wheelchair, confirming Gomez's prediction that he would never walk again. Coleman had been cleaned up and looked hale and hearty, though. All the bruises had faded from his face. Seeing him there like that, free to walk the streets with an arrogant smirk on his face while all his victims were dead and buried, made Braddock's hands clench into fists.

If he'd had a six-gun right now, he would have been sorely tempted to blow both outlaws straight to hell, his own fate be damned. So it was probably a good thing they didn't allow people to be armed in the courtroom.

The judge came in and everybody stood up, Braddock leaning on the cane as he did so. Then the grand jury filed in and took their seats.

Braddock had testified before a grand jury once before, so he knew a little about how the proceedings worked. The district attorney presented the charges against him, then called witnesses, in this case, Coleman and Hawley. Their testimony made it sound like they and their companions had been ambushed by Braddock with no warning and cut down ruthlessly by his shots.

The judge and the jury foreman interrupted now and then to ask questions, usually pressing the witnesses for more details. It seemed obvious to Braddock that Coleman and Hawley were lying and he hoped everybody else could see that, too.

Hawley testified with a quaver in his voice, though, and talked about what a rough time of it he'd had with legs that no longer worked and Braddock thought he saw a little sympathy in the eyes of some of the jurors.

That made him seethe inside but he tried not to show it.

Coleman and Hawley were the only witnesses the district attorney had. Then it was Braddock's turn. When he was called to the stand, he started to use his cane, then changed his mind and left it lying on the table. He didn't need it and damned if he was going to pretend that he did. He strode tall and straight to the witness chair.

After the bailiff had sworn him in, Dunaway asked him to tell his version of what had happened down there in the chaparral, about halfway between San Antonio and Corpus Christi.

"I got on the trail of the men who'd robbed the bank in Corpus and killed two people, then followed them into the brasada country," Braddock said. He nodded toward Coleman and Hawley. "Those two and four of their friends."

The outlaws' lawyer immediately objected. "There's no proof that my clients committed any crime," he insisted. "No charges have been filed against them."

"That's because they haven't been taken back to Nueces County where there'd be witnesses to what they did!" Braddock said.

The judge gaveled him to silence. "You're here to answer questions, Mr. Braddock, not to argue," he warned. "Confine yourself to that."

Anger made Braddock breathe a little harder but he clamped his mouth shut and jerked his head in a nod.

"What happened when you pursued those men, Mr. Braddock?" Dunaway asked.

"They must have realized I was on their trail because *they* bushwhacked *me*. They shot my horse out from under me and I barely made it into the brush without getting ventilated. They came after me to try to kill me. I reckon they must've seen my badge and realized I was a Texas Ranger. They knew killing me was the only way they'd get me off their trail."

The other lawyer objected again on grounds of supposition. The judge sustained it but Braddock thought he did so reluctantly.

With Dunaway prompting him, Braddock told the rest of the story, including the javelina. As he testified, he was aware of the badge resting in the breast pocket of his shirt. He seemed to feel it burning through his clothes, although that was impossible, of course. It was just silver. Nothing but inanimate metal. It didn't really glow with the hatred he felt although, sometimes in unguarded moments, he imagined that it did.

When Braddock was finished, the jury foreman said, "Mr. Braddock, when all this occurred, you were a member of the Texas Rangers, is that correct?"

"Yes, sir. A sworn member of Company D of the Frontier Battalion."

"And you believed you were acting in a proper and lawful manner?"

"Yes, sir. Because I was."

The judge said, "We're not dealing with that issue here, Mr. Braddock."

"Sorry, Your Honor," Braddock muttered.

The jury foreman said, "You're aware that no one really knows what happened out there in the brush except you and these other two men? That it's your word against theirs?"

"The word of a Ranger against two murdering owlhoots, yes, sir, I know that."

That led to more outraged yelling by the lawyer for Coleman and Hawley. Braddock was sick of the whole business. He just wanted to get out of here. He wasn't sure where he would go or what he would do but he was tired of everything being topsy-turvy.

Eventually, the judge dismissed him. The evidence had been presented. There were no closing statements by the lawyers. The grand jury just headed off to figure out whether to indict Braddock on the charges and bind him over for a real trial.

Everybody else waited in the hall outside the courtroom.

Captain Hughes was there. He shook Braddock's hand and said, "How did it go in there?"

"I just told the truth, Captain."

Hughes nodded. "I don't doubt it. Anybody who knew your father would know you're an honest man, G.W."

Braddock's lips thinned. Captain Hughes had treated him decently. Had gone beyond that, really. It wouldn't serve any point to tell him what a dyed-in-the-wool bastard the senior Braddock had really been.

It seemed like the hearing had been over for only a few minutes when the bailiff called them back in. Clearly, it hadn't taken the jury members very long to figure out what they wanted to do.

The announcement was short and to the point, without any real drama to it. The foreman informed the judge that the jury was declining to present a true bill of indictment against George Washington Braddock, Jr. The judge nodded, said, "All charges against the defendant are dismissed," and whacked his gavel on the bench in front of him. "You're free to go, Mr. Braddock."

Dunaway grinned and shook Braddock's hand. Braddock didn't pay any attention to whatever the lawyer was saying. He looked past Dunaway at Coleman and Hawley, both of whom were stony-faced. Braddock saw the hate burning in their eyes, though, as they returned his stare.

He reckoned they saw the same thing in his gaze.

It would always be there.

———

A FEW DAYS after the grand jury hearing, Captain Hughes came into the livery stable a couple of blocks from the Alamo while Braddock was getting his horse ready to ride. The scar on Braddock's back where Tull Coleman had cut him twinged a little as Braddock lifted the saddle onto the back of the dun he had purchased but he ignored the discomfort.

"I heard you were leaving town, G.W.," Hughes said.

"Nothing to keep me here, is there? Now that I'm not a Ranger anymore, I mean."

"Do you have any work lined up?"

Braddock pulled the cinch tight and shook his head. "Not a bit."

"Where are you going?"

"Figured I'd drift west. See what turns up."

"That's not much of a plan," Hughes said with a worried frown.

"I never really had a plan except to carry a badge and enforce the law. Seems like that's over and done with now."

With a note of exasperation in his voice, Hughes said, "I told you, once the legislature passes a new law authorizing the expansion of the Rangers, you might be able to join up again."

"And when will that be, Captain?" Braddock wanted to know.

"Well, there's no telling," Hughes had to admit. "You know it takes a long time for things to go through channels and, like we talked about before, there'll be political enemies trying to stall anything that helps the Rangers."

"So maybe never," Braddock said dryly. "Blind hope doesn't sound like much of a plan, either, Captain."

"Blast it!" Hughes burst out. That was pretty strong language for him and showed that he was genuinely upset. "I know how these things go. I've seen it before. A man rides on one side of the law and then something bad happens and he drifts over to the other side."

Braddock looked at the older man in surprise. "Captain, are you worried that I might turn owlhoot?"

"Things like that have been known to happen," Hughes said stiffly.

Braddock shook his head and said, "You don't have to worry about that. I was brought up my whole life to respect the law."

Even if I didn't respect all the men who enforced it.

"That's not going to change now. I'll never side with the owlhoots. Being a lawman is all I know."

"Well...maybe you can get a job as a deputy somewhere. Texas has settled down a lot but there are still some rough places where a man like you could do some real good, G.W."

"I intend to do good," Braddock said. He meant every word of it, too. He pulled his Winchester part of the way out of the saddle boot to make sure it wasn't catching on anything, then slid it back in. He checked the pack of food and supplies tied on behind the saddle and nodded in satisfaction. His saddlebags were packed with things he would need, too, and a pair of full canteens hung from the saddle. As far as he could tell, he was ready to ride. "If there's nothing else, Captain...?"

"No, that's all." Hughes held out his hand. "Except to wish you good luck."

"Won't need it but I appreciate that."

Braddock gripped the captain's hand and then swung up into the saddle. He lifted a hand in farewell as he rode out of the stable and turned the horse west.

San Antonio was such a big city it took him a while to reach the outskirts. Finally, he put it behind him and started through the wooded hills that rose to the west and north. He paused on a rise and looked back but realized he wasn't leaving anything important behind him. He had everything he needed with him.

Including his badge, and when he thought about it he rested his hand briefly on his shirt pocket, smiling as he felt the hard shape under the cloth. The Rangers might not have any use for him anymore...

But that didn't mean he was through with the Rangers.

5

CROCKETT COUNTY, TEXAS, TWO MONTHS
LATER

MORE THAN THIRTY YEARS EARLIER, THE
transcontinental railroad had been completed with the
driving of the Golden Spike at Promontory Point,
Utah, and, in the decades since then, the steel rails had
spread out in a network that covered much of the
territory west of the Mississippi.

The railroad hadn't come to Crockett County,
though. The nearest rail line was the Southern Pacific,
which ran through Comstock, sixty miles south of
Ozona, which was not only the county seat but also
the only settlement in Crockett County. But the
Deaton Stagecoach Line ran from Ozona to
Comstock, the line's Concord coaches making several
trips back and forth each week. Comstock wasn't far
from the Rio Grande and the terrain around it was
mostly flat but, as the stage road ran north toward
Ozona, it entered more rugged territory marked by

limestone ridges covered with scrub brush, cactus, and mesquite trees.

Today, a southbound coach had just gone through a gap in one of those ridges. The gray-bearded jehu, Ben Finley, kept the team of six sturdy horses at a steady, ground-eating trot. Finley knew better than to run the horses. At best, George Deaton, the line's owner, would dock a driver's pay if he found out the man had been running the teams. At worst, the driver would find himself quickly out of a job. That was understandable since those horses were the life's blood of the company.

Still, there were always special circumstances. This was one of them, Ben Finley realized as he heard gunshots over the pounding of the horses' hooves and looked back to see several riders galloping after the stagecoach. He knew they must have been hidden in the clump of boulders just south of the gap.

Finley shouted at the horses and slashed the long reins across the rumps of the wheelers. The team lunged ahead, jolting the coach and making it rock violently on the broad leather thoroughbraces that supported it. Shouts of alarm came from inside the coach.

Finley had five passengers on this run: two whiskey drummers with orders to fill from Ozona's numerous saloons, a young woman of dubious reputation, a young cowboy who had spent the trip so far ogling the soiled dove, and Rudolph March, a Crockett County rancher on his way to Comstock to catch the train to El Paso where he intended to conduct some business. Finley had toted enough such passengers in his years driving a stagecoach that he felt like he knew all these people, whether he had ever seen them before or not.

"Hold on, folks!" he yelled back at them. "It's liable to get a mite rough!"

That was putting it mildly. The stagecoach road was in pretty good shape because the Deaton family kept it maintained but ruts were inevitable and a coach traveling this fast was going to feel each and every one of them. Finley bounced on the seat as the vehicle careened along.

He had an old Colt Navy .36 in a crossdraw holster on his left side and he wished he could pull the gun and turn around to blaze away at the pursuers. That might discourage them. He wished George Deaton paid somebody to ride shotgun on his coaches, too, but that seemed like an unnecessary expense to the boss. Nobody had tried to hold up one of these coaches in years.

But it was happening today and Finley felt his heart thud in fear as he glanced back and saw the horsebackers gaining on him. They had their hats pulled low and bandannas over their faces, so that seemed to answer any questions about whether or not they were bandits out to hold up the stage.

More shots boomed, closer this time, and Finley twisted around to see the young cowboy hanging out the coach's window and firing back at the outlaws. The cowboy's body jerked suddenly as the gun slipped from his fingers. He slumped forward, his arms hanging down and his head and shoulders still outside the window while the rest of him remained in the coach. Finley could tell by the way youngster's arms swayed limply that he'd been hit and probably was dead.

The jehu bit back a curse and lashed the horses again. The same fate that cowpoke had suffered might be waiting for all of them if they didn't get away.

The road curved around more boulders up ahead, so Finley didn't see the men waiting there for the stagecoach until it was too late. They spurred their horses out into the open, firing as they came, and Finley was driven back against the coach by the slugs pounding into his body. The reins slipped from his fingers as pain flooded through him. Knowing that he was only moments away from death, he clawed at the Colt. He wanted to take at least one of the bastards with him when he crossed the divide.

Instead, he passed out and slid down onto the floorboards to die there. The team kept running until one of the men on horseback caught up to the leaders and leaned over from his saddle to grab the harness and haul back on it. The horses slowed and gradually came to a stop.

The other riders had caught up by now. They all surrounded the coach. A shot blasted from inside the vehicle as Rudolph March put up a fight. After carving out a living on the Texas frontier for so many years, it was all the old rancher knew how to do.

He paid for that stubborn resolve with his life as the outlaws opened fire and hammered the coach with their lead. The thin walls didn't stop very many of the slugs. March fell back out of the window as blood spouted from the holes in his chest. The two drummers screamed even louder than the whore as they tried to hug the floor and escape the storm of bullets.

After a few seconds, one of the bandits waved an arm and shouted an order over the gun-thunder. "Hold your fire! Stop shooting, damn it!"

The guns fell silent as their echoes rolled away over

the hills. The leader motioned to one of the other men and said, "Open that door, Wiley."

Cautiously, the outlaw approached the stagecoach, leaned over from his saddle, and twisted the handle on the door. As he flung it open, a body that was slumped against it inside toppled out, sliding all the way to the ground. The whiskey drummer landed on his back with his arms outflung, his sightless eyes staring at the sky. The front of his vest and shirt were sodden with blood.

"Don't shoot! Oh, God, please don't shoot!"

The plea came from the other drummer. The leader of the outlaws pointed his gun at the open door and ordered, "Come on out of there."

The surviving drummer crawled out of the coach and clung to the door for support as his rubbery legs threatened to fold up underneath him. He was pale and sweating but didn't appear to be wounded.

"Anybody else in there?" the boss outlaw demanded.

"Only a girl...a...a whore...and she's dead."

The boss inclined his head toward the coach and said, "Make sure he's telling the truth."

A couple of the bandits dismounted, grabbed the quaking drummer, and flung him to the ground several yards away from the coach. Then, as one of them leaned into the vehicle through the door, a pop sounded. The man jerked back and yelled a curse. He clapped a hand to his left ear. Blood ran between the fingers.

"Bitch's got a derringer! She damn near shot my ear off!"

The gun must have been a single-shot weapon. The wounded outlaw reached into the coach and dragged out the screaming, struggling soiled dove. He dumped her on the ground next to the dead drummer.

"So she's dead, is she?" the leader said to the surviving drummer. "She looks mighty alive to me."

He raised his gun as the drummer frantically tried to scoot backward on his butt. He yelled, "No! No!" but it didn't do any good. The leader's gun roared and the drummer's head snapped back as a red-rimmed hole appeared in his forehead. He collapsed and didn't move again.

The boss outlaw holstered his gun and then pulled down the bandanna mask over the lower half of his face revealing his lean, beard-stubbled features. He smiled as he said, "We'll take the girl with us. A little extra loot."

The man whose ear had been mangled said, "I oughta get first turn with her. I'm the one she shot."

"I don't know," the boss said with a grin. "You might be too ugly now. Might offend her delicate sensibilities. But I'll think about it." He turned to the others. "Get the box down and bust it open. We'll see what we find. I know March is carrying some money. He was talking in the saloon in Ozona about how he planned to buy some prime bulls from a rancher in Mexico. However much we get, it's a good start."

He dismounted and went over to the young woman. She cowered away from him but he bent down, grasped her arm, and jerked her to her feet. His fingers dug cruelly into her flesh through her sleeve and made her wince.

"Don't give us any more trouble and you'll come through this a whole lot better," he warned her. "I'm not saying you'll enjoy it but it'll be a lot less painful."

"I...I'll do whatever you say, mister," she stammered. "Just don't kill me."

"Why, shoot, you'll be fine," he said as he smiled down at her. "I give you my word on that. And everybody knows you can take ol' Tull Coleman at his word."

6

BRADDOCK RODE INTO OZONA WHILE THE TOWN WAS IN
a hot, sleepy, midday haze. Folks had retreated into the
mostly adobe buildings in search of relative coolness.
Nothing moved on the street except the tails of a few
horses tied at hitch rails as they tried to swat away
flies. Braddock angled his dun toward one of those
rails in front of the Splendid Saloon.

He hoped the place lived up to its name but he
wasn't counting on it.

He was leaner, his features more drawn since the
day he rode away from San Antonio nine weeks
earlier. In that time, he had drifted around considerably, visiting Eagle Pass and Del Rio, then swinging
north to San Angelo and Abilene, back around to
Brownwood, Kerrville, and Bandera, making a wide
circle through southwestern Texas. During that time,
he had kept his ears open, buying dozens of beers,
asking questions, listening to what anybody had to say.

He hoped that effort was about to pay off.

He went into the saloon and thumbed back his hat

as he stood at the bar that ran down the right side of the room. There were a dozen men in the place, half of them engaged in a desultory poker game at a big round table. Two of the others sat at a table nursing drinks, while the other four leaned on the bar and argued without much enthusiasm about the results of a recent horse race.

A craggy-faced bartender drifted along the hardwood until he was across from Braddock. "Get you something, mister?" he asked.

"Beer's fine," Braddock said.

The bartender filled a mug and set it in front of Braddock, who slid a silver dollar across the mahogany.

"Beer's only four bits," the bartender said.

"I'm paying for the company," Braddock said.

The bartender grunted. "Trust me, it ain't worth that much. You ridin' the grub line?"

"What makes you think that?"

"You look like you know your way around cows," the man replied with a shrug. "And you're not from around here. I'd remember you if you were."

"I can set a horse but I've never worked cows in my life," Braddock answered honestly. The only job he'd ever had was as a lawman.

The bartender swiped a rag over the hardwood and said, "Well, it's none of my business."

Sensing the man was about to turn away, Braddock said, "I heard you had some trouble around here not long ago."

"Here in Ozona, you mean? I don't recollect any."

"I'm talking about the stage holdup between here and Comstock. It's got folks in this part of the country stirred up."

"Oh." The bartender nodded. "Well, that's true enough, I suppose. That was a bad thing. A mighty bad thing."

"Outlaws killed the driver and all the passengers on the stage, is that right? Something like six people in all?"

"Yeah." The bartender blew out his breath in a disgusted sigh. "Took a while for the sheriff's posse to find the body of the gal they carried off and, when they did, I reckon they wished they hadn't. Those bastards tore her up real bad, I heard. Finding her didn't do a thing for her, just gave some of those possemen nightmares."

"They were able to give her a decent burial," Braddock pointed out.

"Yeah, there's that, I suppose. But I wouldn't have wanted to see what they did to her."

"The sheriff couldn't trail the men who were responsible for what happened?"

"He tried but to tell you the truth, after seein' the way they slaughtered those folks, I'm not sure he was too keen on catchin' up to 'em, if you know what I mean."

Braddock nodded and sipped the beer that was surprisingly cool.

The bartender grinned. "Good, ain't it? We've got an ice house here in town. I keep my kegs sittin' on a block of ice all the time. Coldest beer between San Antonio and El Paso."

"Splendid," Braddock said dryly. That just made the bartender's grin get bigger. It disappeared, though when Braddock went on, "Have you heard any rumors about who might have pulled that stagecoach robbery?"

"Say, you're mighty interested in that, ain't you?" the bartender asked. "What business is it of yours?"

Braddock reached into his shirt pocket and then laid his hand on the bar. When he turned it up a little, he revealed his badge lying on the hardwood.

The bartender's eyes widened. "Ranger, huh?"

"G.W. Braddock." There was a note of pride in Braddock's voice as he introduced himself.

"I heard the Rangers got put out of business."

"In this world, you hear a lot of things that aren't necessarily true," Braddock said. His tone was flat and hard now. He covered up the badge again and then slipped it back into his pocket. "I know Tull Coleman has put together a new gang and is operating around here. If you have any idea where I might be able to find him, you'd better tell me if you know what's good for you."

"Why in the hell would I know where Tull Coleman is?" the bartender asked. He tried to put some bluster and bravado in his voice but the attempt wasn't very successful. His words were loud enough, though, to draw some attention from the men down the bar.

"I imagine folks from all over this part of the country drink in this saloon. If you keep your ears open, there's no telling what you might hear."

With a surly frown, the bartender said, "A man who keeps his ears open is smart to keep his mouth closed."

Braddock sighed. He had just about run out of patience. He said, "If you've heard anything—"

The bartender didn't let him finish. "Sorry, Ranger. I don't know a damned thing."

If that was the way he wanted to be...

Braddock's left hand shot across the bar. He grabbed the front of the bartender's shirt and twisted, tightening his grip. Then he jerked the man halfway onto the bar, upsetting the mug of beer that sat there. The bartender wasn't a small man but Braddock had taken him by surprise.

The bartender shouted in alarm. Braddock pulled his gun with his other hand and slammed it across the bartender's face, stunning him. Several of the men in the saloon yelled angrily. Braddock maintained his hold on the bartender as he turned and swung his Colt to cover the other patrons.

The two men who'd been drinking at a table were halfway to their feet. The ones playing poker just stared in surprise and confusion. The four men at the bar looked like they wanted to rush Braddock but staring down the barrel of a Colt put a damper on their enthusiasm in a hurry.

"Just stay where you are, gents," Braddock warned. "This is law business."

"Better do what he says," the bartender mumbled. His voice was thick because his lips were swelling where Braddock had hit him. "He's a Ranger."

That brought murmurs of surprise from several of the men. Braddock supposed they had heard the rumors about the Rangers being disbanded, too.

One of the men at the bar said, "I didn't think a Ranger would pistol-whip an innocent man for no good reason."

Braddock let go of the bartender who slid off the hardwood to the floor behind it. He didn't lower the revolver as he said, "When I'm on the trail of murderers, there are no innocent men. I'm looking for the animals who butchered everybody on the Comstock stage and anyone who gets in my way better look out for himself. Best way to do that is to help me find the men I'm after."

The bartender used his rag to wipe blood from his mouth. He said, "Listen, Ranger, a man could get hisself killed telling tales about Tull Coleman."

Mutters of agreement came from some of the other men.

"So he and his bunch *have* been seen around here," Braddock said.

"Nobody's gonna tell you a damned thing," the bartender snapped. "We've all got wives, families."

"What about the men on that stagecoach? Did they have families? What about that woman? She may have been a whore but does that mean she deserved what they did to her?"

Surly silence met Braddock's angry questions but a few of the men at least lowered their eyes as if they were a little ashamed of their reluctance to help him.

That was all right. Braddock hadn't really expected any answers. That wasn't why he'd asked the questions.

Putting a tone of disgust in his voice, he said, "I can see I'm not going to get any help here. I'll just have to find Coleman on my own. But I will. You can damn well count on that."

He backed toward the door and through the batwings before holstering his gun. He jerked the dun's reins loose from the hitch rail and stepped up into the saddle, then turned the horse and rode at a fast lope out of town.

Braddock didn't stop until he was at the top of a small hill just north of Ozona. From here, he could see the entire settlement and the area around it. He dismounted and waited and, less than half an hour later, his patience was rewarded by a thin column of dust curling upward west of town. One rider, by the looks of it, and Braddock could tell that the man was in a hurry.

That was exactly what Braddock expected.

News of the stagecoach robbery had spread quickly probably because the actions of the bandits had been so bloody and brutal. As soon as Braddock had heard that one of the murdered passengers was a well-to-do cattleman who'd been on his way to El Paso with a considerable amount of cash to conduct business, his instincts had told him that Coleman knew Rudolph March would be on that stagecoach.

That meant Coleman had a confederate in Ozona tipping him off. Such an arrangement wasn't uncommon at all. Outlaws ruled by fear and they also had friends and relatives scattered across the country who helped them out. That had been proven time and time again, going all the way back to the days of Jesse James and Sam Bass.

Confident that was the situation here, too, Braddock had gone into Ozona, thrown his weight around, announced that he was a Ranger, and declared his intention of finding Tull Coleman, all for the purpose of spooking whoever was working with Coleman. Braddock had no doubt that the rider he saw raising the dust in the distance was that man.

He reached into his pocket and took out the Ranger badge, pinning it to the front of his shirt. He didn't want anybody mistaking who he was or what he was after.

He was the law and justice was his goal.

He swung up onto the dun and set out after his quarry.

7

THE ROAD RANCH BELONGED TO A MAN CALLED Augustus Vanderslagen, who had given it a name too long and foreign for most folks to remember. So they just called it Dutchman's Folly. Nobody thought the place would last long, out in the middle of nowhere between Ozona and Fort Stockton.

But its sheer isolation proved to be advantageous for those who wanted a place to stop over while they were riding lonely trails and didn't want to draw attention to themselves but desired a drink of decent whiskey, a hot meal, an actual bed, and maybe some female companionship, depending on whether Vanderslagen had any whores working for him at the moment.

Jeff Hawley had been here for several weeks. He spent his days brooding over a chessboard set up on a table in one of the back corners of the low-ceilinged room. He had learned to play as a youngster before the lure of easy money had seduced him into a life of outlawry.

Yeah, easy money, he sometimes thought bitterly. All it had cost him was half of himself. The half that was dead from just above his waist all the way down to his toes, which might as well not have even been there for all the feeling he had in them.

The chess set was missing a black knight and a white bishop. Lord knows what had happened to them. Hawley had talked Rosaria, the young, half-Mexican, half-Comanche whore, into finding a couple of distinctive-looking rocks he used in place of the missing pieces. He leaned forward in his wheelchair and hunched over the board, setting up problems and then working them out, all the while sipping from a glass of tequila that Rosaria refilled now and then. The fiery liquor kept the pain at bay and allowed Hawley to concentrate. At least he *thought* he was concentrating. He wasn't sure but what he was really in a drunken stupor and just didn't know it.

Today, the pain in his back was worse than usual so he'd been drinking more than he normally did. Rosaria watched him from behind the rough bar, which was nothing more than planks laid across whiskey barrels. She was leaning forward so that the low neckline of her blouse drooped enough to reveal practically all of her smooth brown breasts.

Hawley knew she wasn't really trying to be provocative. He might have appreciated the view if he could do anything about it but just like walking, that had ended the day G.W. Braddock put a bullet through his spine. Rosaria had tried every trick she knew to make him a man again—and she knew a lot—but nothing worked. Hawley had given up on that.

A man missing so much from his life had to have *something* to hang on to. With Hawley, it was the determination that one day he would kill that bastard, Braddock.

After staring at the chessboard for a while, he reached out and moved the pink rock that took the place of the white bishop. He was trying to figure out black's best move in response when he heard the swift rataplan of hoofbeats approaching the low, sprawling adobe building.

Behind the bar, Rosaria heard the horse, too. She straightened and looked worried. She and Hawley were the only ones in the barroom. Vanderslagen was in a back room, sleeping off the previous night's sodden binge.

Hawley didn't blame Rosaria for being concerned. A fast horse usually meant trouble. An eighteen-year-old whore and a cripple might be tempting targets for that trouble. It sounded like only one rider was galloping toward Dutchman's Folly, so there was that to be thankful for, at least.

Hawley reached under the blanket that covered his useless legs and brought out a .38 caliber top-break Smith & Wesson revolver with ivory grips. All five chambers in the revolver's cylinder were loaded. Unlike some men, Hawley never worried about carrying the hammer on a live round. If he accidentally shot himself, hell, he'd never feel it, would he? And, if he bled to death, he wouldn't be losing much...other than the chance to have his revenge on the man who had crippled him and it seemed pretty unlikely that would ever come about.

He set the gun on the table next to the chessboard. As bleak as his thoughts were, his situation hadn't completely eroded his natural defiance. If somebody wanted a fight, by God, Jeff Hawley would give him one.

He jerked his head at Rosaria and told her, "Get on in the back."

"I can get the Dutchman's shotgun—"

"No. Just go on back there and don't come out no matter what you hear."

"You're sure?"

"Go, damn it," Hawley told her as the running horse came to a stop outside.

Rosaria scurried out from behind the bar, went past him, and disappeared through the beaded curtain over the rear hallway.

Hawley glanced down at the chessboard one last time, muttered, "Oh, hell, of course," and moved a black rook. He put a finger on the white queen and tipped it over. Checkmate.

A man stepped into the open doorway, starkly silhouetted by the late afternoon sunlight behind him.

Hawley relaxed slightly. Anybody out to kill him who was any good wouldn't have made himself such an easy target.

"Hawley? You in there? Good Lord, it's dark as a bear cave in here. Smells about as bad, too."

Leaning back in his wheelchair, Hawley said, "Damn it, Jennings, I nearly shot you. Don't you know better than to come rushing up to a place like that?"

The newcomer walked on into the room. Hawley could see him better now and recognized the stocky figure, the beefy, flushed face. Edgar Jennings owned one of the stores in town. He drank too much, ate too much, and liked money too much. He was also one of Tull's distant relatives by marriage all of which explained his willingness to help out the gang by providing information. He was the one who had told Hawley about Rudolph March's business trip to El Paso.

"What are you doin' out here?" Hawley went on. "If you've got some other tip you want me to pass on, it's too soon. Tull said he wanted to lay low for a few weeks after hittin' that stagecoach."

Jennings shook his head and said, "No, it's nothing like that. A man rode into town today looking for Tull. He started asking questions in the saloon and he roughed up Brodie and waved a gun around."

"Who the hell would do something like that?"

"He said he was a Texas Ranger."

"That's—" Hawley began. He'd been about to say that was crazy before he stopped. He resumed, "There aren't any Rangers anymore. The state did away with 'em." Again he paused. "Well, all but a few..."

Hawley's frown deepened. The Rangers had been chopped down to practically nothing, that was true enough...but from what he'd heard, a few of them remained on the job. He supposed it was possible one of them was trying to pick up Tull's trail.

"What did this fella look like? Did you see him?"

"Yeah, I was playing poker in the Splendid when he came in. He was tall, sort of long and ropy, but tough looking. Had light brown hair and a mustache."

That could have described a lot of men in Texas but it sounded like one in particular to Hawley, one he had very good reason to know—and hate.

"Now, I'm sure this is loco," he said. "That's G.W. Braddock. He's not a Ranger anymore. I am pure-dee certain of that, Edgar."

Jennings shrugged and said, "I'm just telling you

53

what happened." He frowned. "Braddock...ain't he the one who—"

"Yeah," Hawley cut in. He gripped his chair's wheels and rolled it back from the table. "If he's going around telling people he's a Ranger, he's lying. That damn grand jury wouldn't indict him but he lost his badge, no doubt about that."

"Brodie says he saw the badge."

Hawley scrubbed a hand over his face. Thoughts wheeled crazily through his brain. This didn't make any sense. Had Braddock gotten back into the Rangers somehow? Or was he just pretending to be a lawman?

And the most important question of all...

Where the hell was he now?

"What happened after that dust-up in the saloon?" Hawley snapped. "Where did he go?"

"Hell, I don't know. He rode out of Ozona heading north."

Hawley thought about the terrain around the settlement and, as he did, his worry grew.

"There's a hill up there where Braddock could watch the town," he said. "If that's what he did, there's a good chance he saw you ride out, Edgar."

Jennings' eyes got big with alarm. "You think that's what he did? Son of a bitch! He could have followed me. He could have...could..."

As his voice trailed off, Jennings started shaking his head and backing away.

"Yeah," Hawley said coldly, "he could have."

He picked up the Smith & Wesson and, as rage flooded through him, he fired the revolver five times, emptying its cylinder. Jennings jerked every time one of the .38 caliber slugs punched into his chest. He took a step back, then another, then swayed from side to side as crimson threads of blood trickled from both corners of his mouth. He whimpered once like an animal in pain before he toppled over, upsetting an empty table and a couple of chairs. His face scraped along the rough, splintery planks of the floor, leaving a bloody welt on his cheek, but he never felt it.

Because of the low ceiling, the shots sounded even louder than usual. Hawley's ears rang. He looked down at the empty gun in his hand and realized how his anger had made him stupid. He couldn't hear very well and the revolver was just a useless hunk of metal when it didn't have any bullets in it. He broke it open from the top, dumped the empty brass on the table, and fumbled in the pocket of his vest for fresh rounds.

"Bad idea, Jeff," a voice said, sounding muffled because Hawley's ears were still affected by the shots but clear enough to understand. Two figures moved around the table into Hawley's line of sight. One of them was Rosaria.

The other was G.W. Braddock and he had his left arm looped around the whore's neck, holding her tightly against him. His other hand held a Colt pointed at Hawley.

"You're not..." Hawley began. "You can't be..."

Braddock pulled Rosaria to the side enough to reveal the star-in-a-circle badge pinned to his shirt.

"That's right," he said. "A Texas Ranger."

8

ONCE BRADDOCK WAS REASONABLY SURE THE MAN HE had followed from Ozona was heading toward the lonely adobe building, he swung off the trail and circled wide to come up on the place from the rear.

It looked like the center part of the building had been constructed first, with a few extra rooms added on around it in a haphazard fashion. There was a pole corral in back as well as a long, crude shed where any horses in the corral could get out of the brutal sun. Set at an angle away from the rear corner of the building was a privy.

The corral held only two horses, at the moment, and neither of them paid any attention to Braddock as he rode up. There was a back door but no windows on this side of the building. Braddock didn't even see any loopholes in the wall through which rifles could be fired to defend the place.

That wasn't important anymore, he reminded himself. Indians hadn't caused any trouble in this part of Texas for more than a decade. The only area where renegades were still a problem was out in the Big Bend, where Apaches sometimes raided across the border from their strongholds in the mountains of Mexico.

Like Captain Hughes had said, the Frontier Battalion had done its job too well.

Right now, however, Braddock was glad that whoever owned this place hadn't made it easy to defend. He was able to sneak up on it without being seen.

The back door had a simple string latch. Braddock drew his Colt and used his other hand to unfasten the door. It swung open on leather hinges that had dried out and hardened like iron in this hot, arid climate.

The hallway inside the door was dim and shadowy. Braddock saw some light at the far end where a beaded curtain separated the hall and the main room. A smell of stale beer and whiskey hung in the air. This was a road ranch, Braddock realized, where travelers could stop for a drink or a meal.

It wasn't on a main route, though, which made Braddock think that most of the men who stopped were probably on the dodge from the law. That wouldn't be as lucrative a trade as it once was—again, the Frontier Battalion of the Rangers had been successful at cleaning up a lot of the bandit gangs—but there would always be lawbreakers looking for somewhere to hide out and rest up.

Braddock eased the door closed behind him and started toward the rectangle of light at the far end of the hall. He paused as a raucous snore came from an open door on his right. A grim smile tugged at the corners of his mouth. If whoever was in there was lucky, he would continue sleeping through whatever was about to happen.

A whisper of sound behind him was the only warning he had. He whipped around in a crouch as a figure lunged toward him. There was just enough light in the corridor for him to see a knife coming at him. Braddock ducked and twisted and the blade went harmlessly over his left shoulder. Thrown off balance by the miss, the knife-wielder stumbled against him.

Braddock started to bring his gun down on the attacker's head but he stopped the motion as he realized the body pressed to his was soft and curved, not to mention considerably shorter than him. He wasn't going to pistol-whip a woman.

But he wasn't going to let her stab him, either. As she drew the knife back for another try, he grabbed her wrist and twisted. At the same time, he rammed his Colt back in its holster and clamped that hand over the woman's mouth so she couldn't cry out. He was pretty rough about it, he supposed, but that was better than bashing her head in.

The knife slipped from her fingers and thudded to the floor. Braddock grimaced at the sound but he hoped it went unheard because, by now, men were talking out in the main room. The woman continued to struggle but she stopped when Braddock turned her around and got his left arm around her neck. His forearm pressed against her throat like an iron bar. He could crush her windpipe or even break her neck without much effort and she must have realized that.

He drew his gun again, put his lips against her ear, and whispered, "Just keep quiet and you won't get hurt."

He felt her try to nod. She was agreeing with him.

58

He wasn't going to put any faith in that agreement, though, so he didn't ease up on his hold.

The only thing he had any real faith in was the badge pinned to his shirt.

GEORGE'S FATHER *slapped the little paperbound book on the table and declared, "That's the only Bible you'll ever need right there, son. The Ranger's Bible. The Book of Knaves."*

"The New Testament?" George asked.

The elder Braddock roared with laughter. "Not hardly! That's a list of all the outlaws on our books. We cross 'em off as we bring 'em in...or kill 'em."

"You shouldn't call it a Bible," George said with a frown. "Ma would say that's disrespectful to the Lord's Word."

"Your ma's been gone three years," his pa replied with a snarl. "I never let her tell me what to say or do while she was alive, neither. I sure as hell ain't gonna let some damn button do that."

He started to stand up, obviously expecting George to duck. George didn't, though. Since he'd started to get some growth on him, he'd stopped cringing as much. He figured his pa could still whip him six ways from Sunday if he wanted to but George would deal out some punishment of his own in the process.

George's father pointed a finger at him and said, "One of these days, boy. One of these days you're gonna sass me one too many times and then you'll be sorry."

"I didn't sass you, Pa. I just don't like the idea of calling a list of outlaws a Bible."

"You want truth?" The elder Braddock rested a blunt fingertip on the booklet. "That so-called Good Book up on the shelf is just a bunch of stories. This right here, this is

truth. Bad men, evil men, who'll do anything they want.
They'll steal and they'll kill and they've got to be stopped,
whatever it takes. You want to pray? Pray for the guts to
stand up to those owlhoots, when the time comes for you to
go after them." He shook his head. "I still ain't sure you got
what it takes, boy. Maybe you better forget about bein' a
Ranger. Maybe you better be a preacher instead. Stick to
psalm-singin' and hallelujah-shoutin' with the women while
other men do the real work of bringin' law and order to
Texas. Maybe that's what you're cut out for." Contempt
dripped from his voice as he added, "That'd make your ma
right proud of you."

In the shadowy hallway in the back of the road ranch,
Braddock gave a little shake of his head. Most of the
time he did his best not to think about his father at all
but the old bastard crawled out of his memories now
and then, no matter how hard Braddock tried to
banish him.

The old man had always damned Braddock's ma
for being weak but a couple of times after she died,
Braddock had seen his father staring at an old picture
of his mother and he'd been crying. He would have
denied it, of course, but his eyes had been wet with
tears.

Braddock forced his thoughts back into the
present. He recognized one of the voices in the front
room. It belonged to Jeff Hawley. So Hawley was still
alive, against all odds. That was good because if
anybody would know where to find Tull Coleman, it
was the crippled outlaw.

The girl didn't struggle as he moved closer to the

door and took her with him. It was a little lighter here and he could see her better. She looked mostly Mexican but her high cheekbones made him think she had some Indian blood, too. She was young and fairly attractive but whoring at an owlhoot road ranch like this, those looks wouldn't last very long.

Luckily, that wasn't his problem. Finding Tull Coleman and bringing him to justice was.

Even with Braddock's arm across her throat, the girl let out a little squeal of fright when shots roared in the other room. Braddock tightened his grip on her. He heard a heavy thud that was probably a body falling to the floor. Not Hawley, he hoped. He needed Hawley alive for now. He forced the girl forward, pushing through the beaded curtain while the air in the other room was still full of echoes from the gunshots.

Hawley was sitting in a wheelchair behind a table a few feet away on Braddock's right. Braddock's eyes took in the rest of the scene in a split-second's glance. He saw the corpse lying on the floor in an ungainly sprawl and recognized the man as one of the hombres who'd been playing poker in the Splendid Saloon back in Ozona. That fit right in with his theory about one of the local citizens working with Coleman's gang.

He saw Hawley trying to reload the Smith & Wesson .38 he'd just emptied. Braddock moved on out into the room and said, "Bad idea, Jeff."

Hawley gaped at him in astonishment. "You're not...you can't be..."

Braddock pulled the girl aside so Hawley could see the badge. "That's right. A Texas Ranger."

"But they kicked you out of the Rangers!"

Braddock smiled slowly. Let Hawley make of that whatever he would.

"All the Rangers are gone except for a few..."

Hawley's voice faded as he looked down at the broken-open revolver in his right hand. He held a fresh cartridge in his left hand. Braddock could tell what Hawley was thinking just as clearly as if it had been written down in a book.

The Book of Knaves.

"You're wondering how quick you could put that bullet in the cylinder, close it, and take a shot at me, aren't you, Jeff? You'd have to be mighty fast for it to do any good. How steady are your hands? Is that tequila in your glass? You really think you could even get a shot off before I blow a few holes through you."

"You crippled me. You shot me in the back, you damn coward."

"You'd just tried to kill me and I didn't want you to get away."

"I swore I'd kill you," Hawley said as he looked down at the gun. "Even if it costs me my life." He raised his eyes and stared at Braddock. "You think I really care if I live or die anymore?"

Braddock saw the resolve in the outlaw's eyes and knew he was going to have to shoot Hawley. He figured he would put a bullet through the man's shoulder—both shoulders if he had to—so that Hawley could still talk.

That was when a big, sloppy figure burst through the beaded curtain behind him, shouted something in a language Braddock didn't understand, pointed a shotgun at him, and pulled the trigger.

9

BRADDOCK'S SWIFT REACTION WAS THE ONLY THING THAT saved both him and the girl. The fat man obviously didn't care if the shotgun blast shredded her, too.

But Braddock dived to the floor before the load of buckshot had time to spread out much. The girl was underneath him with his body shielding hers. The blast went over both of them and blew a jagged hole in one of the whiskey barrels supporting the bar planks. Rotgut spewed out.

The fat man had fired only one barrel which meant he was still dangerous. He wore a nightshirt, the bottom of which flapped around pale calves as big around as the trunks of small trees. The man's head was shaped like a barrel cactus and was bald except for some wildly askew strands of white hair. He kept yelling in that foreign language as he started to lower the shotgun's twin barrels toward Braddock.

Braddock angled his Colt up and fired first. The bullet ripped through the fat man's double chin and plowed on up into his brain. He flopped backward as he triggered the shotgun's second barrel. The charge went harmlessly into the ceiling.

Braddock caught movement from the corner of his eye and turned his head to see Hawley turning over the table and shoving it at him. The chessboard and pieces went flying. The table hit Braddock and didn't do any real damage but it did jolt the gun out of his hand.

With the chair's wheels squealing, Hawley rolled toward Braddock and then dived out of the chair. He landed on top of Braddock and clawed at his throat. Hawley's fingers closed like talons on Braddock's windpipe.

Braddock tried to throw Hawley off but the outlaw clung to him like a leech. As they rolled through the lake of spilled whiskey, they tangled with the girl, who started to scream now that Braddock didn't have hold of her anymore. She raked her fingernails across Braddock's face as she tried to help Hawley overpower him.

Anger surged up inside Braddock. He backhanded the girl and knocked her away from him. Then he hammered a punch into the side of Hawley's head. He had to hit the outlaw twice more before Hawley's grip loosened. Braddock put his hands against Hawley's chest and shoved him away.

Hawley lay there panting. "You...you son of a bitch," he said as Braddock climbed onto his knees and then got to his feet. "You stand there...whole...such a big man." He clenched a fist and pounded it against the floor in frustration as furious tears rolled down his sallow cheeks. "Why don't you come over here and kick me?" he shouted. "Come on! Stomp the helpless cripple!"

"I don't want to stomp you, Hawley," Braddock said.

He bent and picked up the gun he had dropped. A glance toward the fat man told him he didn't have to worry about any more threats from that direction. The man lay on his back with a large pool of blood spreading around his head.

The girl was huddled against one of the whiskey barrels, evidently stunned. Braddock didn't trust her, so he kept a watch on her from the corner of his eye as he pointed the Colt at Hawley.

"What I want is for you to tell me where to find Tull Coleman. And don't try to lie and claim you don't know. Neither of us are foolish enough to believe that."

"You really think I'd tell you?" Hawley asked. "I'd die first and you know that."

"Up to you," Braddock said as he thumbed back the Colt's hammers. Now that the echoes of the earlier shots had died away, the sound was loud in the close confines of the room.

Hawley glared at him for a few seconds, then started to laugh. He propped himself up on one hand and used the other to beckon to Braddock. "Go ahead and shoot," he urged. "Come on, get closer! You don't want to miss, Ranger. Now you be sure to go ahead and kill me this time. Don't foul it up again." He leaned forward. "Come on, you can do it! Just pull that damn trigger if you've got the guts! Or maybe you're too much of a coward to shoot a man who's lookin' you right in the eye."

Hawley's voice wasn't the only one Braddock seemed to hear at that moment. If he hadn't known better, he would have sworn his father was right there behind him, goading him to shoot the outlaw. Braddock Sr.'s voice was weaker now, slurred as it had been in those last days when the sickness was killing him and whiskey was the only thing that would dull the pain. But even on his last legs, he'd been as filled with hate and rage as ever, hatred for outlaws and rage toward the son he thought would never be the man he was.

Braddock listened to both of them, then lowered his gun and slid it back in its holster. He stalked over to Hawley, bent down, and took hold of the outlaw's shirt. He lifted Hawley, who cursed and struck feebly at him. Braddock turned and shoved Hawley into the wheelchair, which rolled backward a little from the impact.

"You're not going anywhere," Braddock said.

Hawley cursed some more, grabbed hold of the chair's arms and tried to shake it in sheer, futile frustration. Then he slumped back and sobbed.

Braddock felt a little sick. There was something repulsive about Hawley. Not his disability so much as it was his reaction to it. The outlaw was like a broken-backed snake, writhing in the dust and biting at things that weren't there.

The girl moaned. Braddock put his hands under her arms and lifted her to her feet. She stood there unsteadily, shaking her head. Finally, she lifted it, looked at Braddock and said, "You hit me."

"I reckon you had it coming. You were trying to help Hawley kill me."

"*You* are the one who has it coming! He was a strong man, and you made him weak."

"He was never strong," Braddock said. "He was a damn outlaw. All he ever did was take advantage of people and hurt them."

Her chin lifted defiantly. "He never hurt me."

"He just hadn't gotten around to it yet." Braddock

changed the subject by asking, "Tull Coleman comes here to see him, doesn't he?"

With a surly glare, she said, "I don't know any Tull Coleman."

Braddock let out an exasperated sigh. "I don't know why everybody feels compelled to lie to help that murdering bastard. What direction does Coleman come from? Just tell me that and I'll go away and leave the two of you alone."

"To do what?" the girl wanted to know. "You killed the Dutchman. This was his place. Now it's nothing."

"Maybe you could run it. You and Hawley."

A shrewd, calculating look replaced the angry expression on her face. "You really think so?"

"Unless that Dutchman, as you call him, has some relatives who can come in and take over everything."

She shook her head slowly and said, "He never said anything about any family."

"Well, there you go," Braddock told her. "What happens here is none of my business. All I care about is finding Coleman."

"If I tell you what I know...you'll drag out that lard-gutted carcass and bury it?"

From the sound of it, she hadn't liked the Dutchman very much. Braddock supposed that he'd treated her pretty roughly.

"Sure," Braddock said. He didn't know if he would keep the promise but he was willing to make it.

The girl hesitated a moment longer, then said, "All right. It's not much but I'll tell you."

Before she could say anything else, Braddock heard wheels creaking. He turned to see Hawley rolling toward them. The outlaw had a grimly determined

67

look on his face but he was unarmed as far as Braddock could see.

Then, he realized Hawley held something in his hand. He lifted it and Braddock saw it was a match. With a flick of his thumbnail, Hawley set the thing alight.

Then he dropped it on the floor in front of him, right into the big pool of whiskey that had leaked out of the buckshot-shattered barrel.

The liquor went up in a huge *whoosh!* of flame that made the girl jump back and scream. Hawley howled with laughter as he rolled forward and the fire engulfed him. His clothes and hair, soaked with whiskey from rolling around in it on the floor, started burning, but he kept laughing.

Braddock grabbed the girl as the flames shot across the floor, following the spilled whiskey, and reached the broken barrel. The liquor that was still in the barrel ignited. It was like a bomb going off, setting the bar on fire and spreading the flames to the other barrels.

Braddock jerked the girl off her feet and dashed toward the door. He slammed through the opening just as more of the barrels exploded behind them.

The force of the blast pushed Braddock forward like a giant hand in his back. He lost his hold on the girl just before he slammed into the ground. As he rolled over, he heard what sounded like thunder but the sky was clear. The rumble came from inside the building where thick clouds of black smoke were now gushing out of every opening.

The adobe walls wouldn't burn very well but the roof and everything inside the place would.

Including Jeff Hawley.

Braddock pushed himself up and looked at the inferno. Even if Hawley hadn't been crippled, he never would have made it out of there alive. He was bound to be dead by now...and he had taken his knowledge of Tull Coleman's whereabouts with him.

That realization put a bitter taste in Braddock's mouth. He climbed wearily to his feet and looked around for his hat and the girl. He spotted them both but picked up his hat first, slapping it against his thigh to get some of the dust off of it before he put it back on.

Then he took hold of the girl's bare arm and lifted her. "Looks like you won't be running this road ranch after all," he muttered. "Time that fire quits burning, there won't be much left."

She spat words at him but they weren't in Spanish or English like he would have expected. They were German, he realized, the same as what the Dutchman had been shouting at him. She must have picked them up from the fat man while she was working for him.

When her fury finally ran out of steam, she demanded, "What will I do now?"

"Tell me where I can find Tull Coleman," Braddock said.

"Do you *never* think of anything else?"

"Not much," Braddock admitted.

They stood there glaring at each other while the building continued to burn. At last, the girl said, "I will tell you what I know, but you must do something for me first."

"What's that?" Braddock asked warily.

"Take me back to the village where I came from. It's just across the border in Mexico, about forty miles south of here."

Braddock frowned. "I don't have time to—"

"There was a man who came to see Señor Jeff every week or ten days. A man lean like you, with reddish hair and a little beard, who was always smiling with his mouth but his eyes were cold like those of a snake."

That was Coleman, Braddock thought. There was no doubt of it in his mind.

"I will tell you which way he came from," the girl went on. "I will tell you everything I heard them talking about...but only after you have taken me back to my home."

"Are you sure you'll be welcome there?" Braddock asked. He knew it was a cruel question and didn't care.

"You mean because I was a whore for the gringos?" She shrugged and that caused her blouse to slide down on one shoulder. "It doesn't matter. I have nowhere else to go...because of you."

"Hawley's the one who set the place on fire." Braddock grunted. "That Dutchman must have had a hell of a lot of whiskey stored in there."

The girl put her hands on her hips. "Do you want my help or not?"

"How do I know I can trust you?"

"If you take me back to my village, I will have nothing to gain by lying to you."

Braddock supposed that was true enough. What she was suggesting would take only a few days and he had the time to spare. He had almost nothing but time.

And his duty.

"All right," he said. "We'll go to Mexico. But there's something you have to tell me first."

She frowned warily at him and asked, "What is that?"

"What the hell is your name?"

She looked a little surprised by the question, but she said, "Rosaria. And I know your name. You are Braddock." She paused. "Braddock the bastard."

Without intending to, he found himself smiling.

"As good a name as any, I suppose," he said.

Rosaria didn't own anything except the clothes she was wearing and all of Braddock's supplies were in his saddlebags or tied on behind his saddle, so they didn't really need the third horse as a pack animal. Braddock brought it along anyway, leading it with a piece of rope he'd found in the shed. There was tack in there, too, so Rosaria didn't have to ride bareback. She'd straddled the saddle without hesitation, pulling her long skirt up to mid-thigh to free her legs.

They rode side by side in silence starting out but the quiet seemed to get on Rosaria's nerves. After a while, she said, "Hawley told me the man who shot him was no longer a Ranger. He said he and his friend tried to use your own law against you."

"Well, it's pretty clear that didn't work, isn't it?" Braddock said. He was still upset that he hadn't been able to force any information out of Hawley before the outlaw died, so he wasn't in much of a mood for small talk.

Rosaria persisted. "How did you get the Rangers to take you back?"

"That's my business," Braddock said. He couldn't explain things to this whore. She'd never understand that it didn't really matter what the State of Texas said. He'd never had anything else in his life except being a Ranger, not really, and nothing could change that. The star-in-a-circle badge *belonged* on his chest. If he put it away, if he gave up the only thing that had ever meant anything to him, it would be the same as admitting that his old man was right.

After a few minutes, she said, "Nobody ever tried to stop me from being a whore. All the men in my village seemed to think that was what I should be, from the time I was twelve years old."

Braddock just grunted. He wasn't interested in hearing her life story, any more than he was in sharing his with her.

"My father is a farmer. All the men in my village are farmers. And they are all poor. I have many brothers and sisters so my father told me, since I was the oldest, I should do whatever I could to help feed them. I did but, after a while, I grew tired of it so I ran away."

"And wound up doing the same thing for the Dutchman," Braddock said, then grimaced because he hadn't meant to encourage her to continue and he knew she would take his comment that way.

"Sí, only it was even worse. Augustus was a cruel man."

"That was his name?" She wasn't going to shut up, Braddock decided, so he might as well talk to her.

"Augustus Vanderslagen. A terrible name, and a terrible man. Do you know why he tried to shoot you?"

"I figured he was trying to help Hawley."

Rosaria shook her head. "No. It was because you woke him up. He always flew into a rage whenever anything disturbed his sleep, especially if he'd been drinking the night before. Once, he chased me all around the place with a meat cleaver because I dropped some empty bottles and woke him. He would have killed me if I hadn't been fast enough to stay out of his reach."

Braddock had to laugh in spite of himself. "I'm glad I shot him, then. I was feeling a little bad about it."

"Were you? Really?"

"Well, no, not much," Braddock admitted. "Once he took a shot at me, I didn't care why. That made him fair game as far as the law's concerned." He paused, then asked, "Why did you stay there, if he treated you so bad?"

Rosaria shrugged, which made her blouse slip again. "Where else could I go where I would be sure of better treatment? Besides, Augustus wasn't always like that, just most of the time. Every now and then he could be nice. It wasn't like I had a lot of choices."

"Most of us don't," Braddock said. "Fate drives us on, wherever it wants us to go."

IT WAS MOSTLY FLAT, open country covered with scrub brush south of Dutchman's Folly all the way to the border, with only occasional ridges and knobs to break the monotony. Late that afternoon, Braddock found a place to camp up against the base of one of those ridges. There was no water nearby but he had a full canteen and most of another one. They would just have to be careful with their water.

Before darkness settled down, he built a small fire to boil some coffee and fry some bacon, then put out the flames. As far as he knew, no one was looking for them but such caution had become an ingrained habit with him. When you were spending the night out in the open, there was no point in announcing where you were.

As they ate their meager supper, Rosaria sighed and said, "I suppose I will have to sleep on the ground tonight."

"I have an extra blanket you can use," Braddock said.

"Or I could share your blankets," she suggested.

He sipped coffee from the tin cup in his hand, then said, "I don't reckon that'd be a good idea."

"Why? Because I'm a common whore? Because you're too good for me?"

"Because I'm not totally convinced you wouldn't try to get my knife and cut my throat while I'm asleep."

She looked at him expressionlessly for a moment, then laughed. "The big, strong Texas Ranger is afraid of a little Mexican girl."

"I just believe in being careful, that's all."

"You're taking me home. Why would I kill you?"

"I figure you know where you're going," Braddock said. "You don't really need my help to get there. If you rode into that village of yours with three horses and all my gear, I reckon that'd make you one of the richest people there."

She laughed again and said, "You are right about that, señor."

"So just to be sure, I'm going to keep my distance from you. No offense."

"No offense," she agreed with a smile. "You are the one who is missing an opportunity, not me."

"Won't be the first one," Braddock said as he looked down into his coffee cup.

"WITH SOME HARD WORK, you could really make something out of your father's spread," Laura McElhaney said as she rested her head on George's shoulder. They were sitting on a bench on her pa's front porch, with silvery moonlight washing over the yard in front of them.

"I don't think I'm cut out to be a rancher," George said. "Pa wasn't, either. It was just a place for Ma and me to stay while he was off Rangering."

"That doesn't mean it has to stay that way," Laura said. "I...I could help you. If...if you had a good woman with you...a wife...Oh, George, I know I'm being mighty forward, but I don't want to see you throw your life away."

George stiffened. "Like my pa threw his life away being a Ranger?"

"That's not what I meant—"

"Good Lord, I only put him in the ground three days ago and you're already telling me to forget everything about him. Forget what he was and what he wanted me to be."

Laura straightened and turned to look intently at him. "That's not what I meant and you know it, George Washington Braddock. But be honest. He bullied you into deciding to join the Rangers and everybody around here knows it."

George stood up and stepped over to the porch railing. "I don't want to hear this."

Laura moved beside him and put her hand on his shoulder. "All I'm saying is your father is gone, rest his soul, and you don't have to follow the trail he laid out for you. You can make up your own mind what to do, George."

"I already have." He drew in a deep breath. "I'm riding up to Austin tomorrow to sign my papers with the Rangers."

"You don't have to do that. You can stay here and work the ranch. And if you were to ask me to work it with you, as your wife, I'd say yes."

He'd been courting her, off and on, for two years, and tonight was the boldest he'd ever seen her. She moved against him, slid one arm around his waist and the other around the back of his neck. He felt her body pressed intimately to his and couldn't help but react.

"You know it's what we both want," she whispered.

What she was saying might be true, George thought, but it didn't really matter. His course had been set for him long before. He had grown up seeing the fear and loneliness in his mother's eyes every time his father rode away and he had sworn to himself that he would never inflict that pain on any woman. His own happiness didn't mean a damned thing when it was stacked up against bringing law and order to the Lone Star State.

He put his hands on Laura's shoulders and moved her away from him. "I'm sorry," he said as he turned toward the porch steps. "I just came by tonight to say goodbye."

"George, you can't just throw away—"

"Goodbye, Laura," he said.

He walked away and didn't look back, even though he heard her sobbing behind him. The easiest thing in the world would have been to turn around and run back to her.

But Rangers didn't do things the easy way.

They did things the right way.

BRADDOCK GAVE Rosaria the extra blanket and told her to bed down on the other side of the dead campfire. While she was doing that he checked the horses one last time, then sat down with his back against a rock and the Winchester close beside him on the ground.

"Aren't you going to sleep?" she asked from where she lay curled up in the blanket.

"Maybe later," Braddock said. "I thought I'd stay awake for a while."

"Why? There are no hostile Indians out here and the odds of any bandits running across us are small."

"I just like to be careful, that's all."

"A man can be careful all his life and still have trouble come at him when he least expects it."

Braddock thought about what had happened in San Antonio when he brought in Tull Coleman and Jeff Hawley. There was no way he could have anticipated the news about the Rangers being disbanded or predicted the effects that development would have. So Rosaria might be right, he mused, but he still couldn't change what he was.

"Just go to sleep and don't worry about me," he told her.

"I don't worry about you," she said. She yawned sleepily. "I don't give a damn about you, Ranger."

Good, he thought. That was just the way he wanted it.

SAN ANTONIO

RANGER HEADQUARTERS WAS MIGHTY QUIET THESE DAYS. The organization had been cut down to four "companies", if you could call them that, of six men each— three officers and three privates. Captain Hughes was still in command of Company D. His clerk had always been one of the Rangers in the company but now the man was a civilian employee.

The clerk brought in a piece of paper and placed it on Hughes' desk. "Got a letter here for you, Cap'n, from the sheriff of Crockett County over in Ozona."

"He's not complaining because I haven't been able to give him any help tracking down those stagecoach robbers, I hope," Hughes said as he put aside the report he'd been reading and picked up the letter instead.

"Ah...no, sir. He's complainin' because the man you sent roughed up one of his citizens and threatened some more of 'em."

"What?" Hughes frowned. "I didn't send a Ranger to Ozona."

The clerk gestured toward the letter and said, "Not accordin' to that."

Hughes glared through his spectacles and his frown deepened as he read. His fingers clenched involuntarily on the paper, making it crackle.

"Braddock!" he said. "G.W. Braddock's going around telling people he's still a Texas Ranger?"

"Showin' folks the badge and everything, accordin' to the sheriff in Ozona," the clerk said.

Hughes slapped the letter down on the desk and came to his feet. "We can't allow this," he said. "He's not only pretending to be a Ranger, that says he pistol-whipped an innocent man! Braddock must have lost his mind."

"Sounds plumb loco, all right," the clerk agreed.

"He has to be stopped. He'll have to be brought in so he can't keep doing this." Hughes sighed. "The fool. The blasted young fool. I was afraid this would happen. Doesn't he realize that by adopting this...this masquerade, he's put himself on the wrong side of the law?"

"He's tryin' to hunt down Tull Coleman and his bunch, Cap'n. You said yourself when you heard about that stagecoach robbery and all the killin' that went with it, that it sounded like Coleman's dirty work."

"And I don't doubt for a second that it was but Braddock has no legal authority to go after them. By doing so, especially the way he's doing it..." Hughes paused and shook his head. "I hate to say it but G.W. Braddock has made himself an outlaw."

THE MAN CALLED Wiley was with Coleman as they approached Dutchman's Folly. Everything looked normal from a distance but, as they came closer, Coleman noticed that some of the walls had a blackened look to them. A couple of poles had been knocked down in the corral and the enclosure was empty.

Coleman reined in and said, "Something's wrong."

Wiley brought his horse to a stop as well and asked, "What do you mean, boss?"

"It looks like there's been a fire inside the building. Let me get my spyglass out..."

Coleman took a brass telescope from his saddlebags and pulled it out to its full length. He had taken the instrument from the body of an army officer he had killed several years earlier. The two of them had gotten into a disagreement over a whore at a saloon in Sweetwater. Coleman had had to back down because the son of a bitch had some friends with him but he'd bided his time and, a couple of nights later, had caught the man in an alley and put a Bowie knife in his back.

Now Coleman squinted through the glass for a moment and said, "Yeah, the roof's burned and fallen in, looks like. I don't see anything moving around the place."

"What do you think happened to Hawley?"

"I intend to find out." Coleman closed the telescope with a snap and stowed it away, then pulled his Winchester from its saddle boot and nudged his horse into motion again.

Both outlaws had their rifles out and were ready for trouble as they rode up to the building. A couple of black-winged buzzards rose from inside the walls, flying up through where the roof had been, and started flapping lazily away.

"Filthy scavengers," Coleman snarled. He brought the Winchester to his shoulder and fired. Feathers flew and one of the buzzards dropped like a stone. The other bird tried to wheel away but Coleman worked the rifle's lever, shifted his aim, and downed it, too. The shots were loud in the silence that hung over the deserted and destroyed road ranch.

"I don't much like this, Tull," Wiley said nervously.

"Stay out here, then, if you want to," Coleman said. He swung a leg over his saddle and slid to the ground, landing gracefully with his rifle still ready for instant use. As he strode toward where the door had been, he said without looking around, "I'm going to see if I can figure out what happened here."

Tumbled heaps of ashes were everywhere inside the building. The fire must have been fierce while it was burning but everything was cold now. Coleman figured the place must have burned days earlier. The smell still hung in the air but that would take a long time to go away.

Little gray clouds rose around Coleman's legs as he kicked his way through the debris. One of his feet hit something solid, metallic. He pushed some ashes aside, bent and picked up whatever it was he had found, frowning as he tried to figure it out. After a moment he said aloud, "It's a wheel hub."

"What'd you say, boss?" Wiley called from outside.

Coleman ignored him. He kicked around some more and uncovered another wheel hub and some charred remnants of what looked like a chair. Then his foot thudded against something else that rolled.

Coleman recoiled as he realized he was looking down at a human skull that grinned up at him.

"Son of a..." Coleman started to drag in a deep breath, then stopped as he realized he would be breathing ashes and God knew what else. He poked around and found more bones, then straightened and sighed.

He knew he was looking at what remained of his friend Jeff Hawley.

A fire of anger as hot as the conflagration that had consumed Dutchman's Folly began to blaze inside Coleman. He and Hawley had ridden together for several years. Hawley had been the only one left from Coleman's original gang, and even though he couldn't ride with the rest of the boys anymore, Coleman still considered him one of the bunch. Hawley had proven his worth by acting as the go-between for the friends and relatives in the area who fed information to Coleman.

Now he had died, probably in agony as the flames writhed around him and Coleman wanted to know whether his friend's death was an accident...or if it had been deliberate. Jeff had already suffered so much, being crippled by that damned Ranger's bullet. He hadn't deserved this, too.

Coleman searched through the rest of the devastation and found another charred skeleton lying several yards away from Hawley's. When he turned the skull over, he saw the gaping hole in the back of it. That was where a bullet had exploded out, Coleman decided. Whoever this was—the Dutchman, maybe?—he'd been shot.

As far as Coleman was concerned, that did away with any possibility of the fire being accidental.

Someone had done this. Coleman was determined to find out who and wreak his vengeance on them.

"You all right in there, Tull?" Wiley called.

"No, I'm not all right," Coleman snapped. "Jeff's dead. What's left of him is in here."

"Son of a bitch," Wiley said. His hushed tone made the words sound more like a prayer than a curse. "I found somethin' out here you might oughta take a look at."

Coleman glanced at Hawley's remains. There was nothing else he could do for his friend, not here, anyway. He walked out of the burned building and stomped his feet on the hard ground to get as many ashes off his boots and trouser legs as he could.

"What is it?" he asked Wiley.

"Well, I decided to take a look around out here while you were lookin' in there," Wiley said. He was a tall, burly man with a beard and long, tangled dark hair that fell to his shoulders under a tightly curled Stetson. He pointed and went on, "I found some tracks over yonder."

Coleman's pulse sped up. Tracks might have been left by whoever was responsible for this.

"Show me," he said.

Wiley led him over to the hoofprints. They were several days old, just like the destruction in the road ranch, but it hadn't rained and there hadn't been much wind, so the tracks were still fairly clear.

"Three horses, two of 'em carryin' riders and one that wasn't," Wiley said. "I backtracked 'em around to the corral. I'd say somebody tied a mount around there, then took down a couple of poles and got the other horses out. I looked for boot prints but couldn't really make heads or tails of what I found."

"That's all right," Coleman said. "You did good anyway. I'll bet that whoever killed Jeff and set the place on fire took those horses. And then they headed south." He gazed off in that direction, his eyes hooded against the sun glare, as he continued, "Go on back to the hide-out and get the rest of the boys. Then come back here and pick up the trail."

"What're you gonna do, Tull?"

"I'm starting after the bastards now," Coleman said. "I don't know who they are but I'm going to make them pay for what they did to Jeff."

1 2

"Does this place have a name?" Braddock asked as he and Rosaria rode toward the scattered gathering of adobe jacals. He saw a cantina, a blacksmith shop, and what appeared to be a small store. At the far end of the open area that passed for a street was the largest building in town, a church with a short, blocky bell tower. Next to the church was a well.

Fields with scrawny crops in them surrounded the settlement. Irrigation ditches led from the fields to the Rio Grande, which was a quarter of a mile to the north.

"It is called *La Catedral de la Esperanza,*" Rosaria said in reply to Braddock's question. "The Cathedral of Hope, after the church. But everyone usually just calls it Esperanza."

"Looks more like No Hope to me," Braddock said with a wry smile.

"I told you that I was eager to get away from here when I left. What did you expect?"

Braddock didn't answer her question. He said, "Let's just get you back to your family so you can tell me what I need to know and I can be on my way."

The ride from Dutchman's Folly had taken them two full days, plus the remainder of the day they had started out. That meant two nights on the trail. Braddock hadn't slept much either night, just dozed some now and then, because he didn't fully trust Rosaria. She had tried to stab him and then fought on Hawley's side against him. He didn't believe she had miraculously become his friend.

On the other hand, he was the only one around to help her, and he had a hunch Rosaria was pretty damned practical. Like most people in the world, she would use anybody she had to in order to get what she wanted.

At least she had given up trying to coax her way into his blankets at night. She had made some comments in German that he had taken to be pretty derogatory toward his manhood but things like that didn't bother him. He had more important matters to worry about.

Like finding Tull Cameron and bringing him to justice.

"My father's house is this way," Rosaria said as she led him toward one of the huts on the far side of the village. It wasn't long until nightfall. Men and women were trudging back in from the fields, their shoulders drooping with weariness.

Nearly a dozen small children came running, trailed by several barking dogs, as Braddock and Rosaria rode up to one of the jacals. The youngsters shouted Rosaria's name, leading Braddock to think they must be those younger brothers and sisters she had talked about. She dismounted and began embracing them as they hugged her eagerly in return.

Braddock surprised himself a little by realizing he was glad the homecoming was a happy one for her. Sure, she had tried to kill him but he supposed that, under the circumstances, he could understand. She hadn't known who he was when she tried to stick a knife in his back. He was just a tough-looking stranger with a gun, evidently intent on disrupting her life.

And sure enough, things had played out that way.

But maybe she would be better off now in the long run. She hadn't had much of a future waiting for her at Dutchman's Folly.

A tired-looking woman walked up and exclaimed, "Rosaria!" A torrent of rapid Spanish passed between them. Like most folks in Texas, especially the southern half of the state, Braddock had some understanding of Spanish but the two women were going 'way too fast for him to keep up.

The older woman didn't seem happy to see Rosaria. She waved her hands in the air and practically spat out her words. After a few minutes of agitated conversation, Rosaria sighed and turned back to Braddock.

"My father is dead," she said.

"I'm sorry," Braddock told her. "I lost my pa a few years ago."

"My father was not a particularly good man but I'm sorry he worked himself to death. And now my mother doesn't want me here. She says I have brought shame to the family."

Braddock wanted her to go ahead and honor her part of the bargain, to tell him whatever she could about the visits Tull Coleman had paid to Hawley at

Dutchman's Folly so he could be on his way. However, it was really too late in the day for him to start north again, and since it looked like he'd be spending the night here in Esperanza he supposed it wouldn't hurt anything for him to be sympathetic. He said, "I guess you can stay somewhere else."

"There is nowhere else," Rosaria said with a bleak look on her face. "Maybe I could go to the cantina and do the same things there I did before. The same things I did for the Dutchman. But I had hoped—" She stopped short and laughed bitterly. "You are right, Braddock. This place should be called No Hope."

His jaw tightened. He felt sorry for her and he didn't want that. Such an emotion would just interfere with his quest to bring Coleman to justice. He had already spent too much time helping out Rosaria.

"I will go with you," she announced.

"What?" Braddock frowned. "Go with me where? I brought you where you wanted to go."

"But there is nothing here for me. Take me with you, and I will help you find the man you're looking for. The outlaw called Tull Coleman. I can show you the trail he followed when he came to the Dutchman's place."

"You can *tell* me where that trail is," Braddock said. "That was our deal. Nothing was ever said about you coming with me after this."

She shrugged. "Things have changed."

Braddock was so exasperated, he felt like turning his horse around and galloping away from here, taking the two extra mounts with him. Since he would have fresh horses he could switch to, he could maintain a fast pace as he rode north again through Texas. He could be back where he'd started in less than two days, he estimated.

But if he did that...he'd be back where he started. No closer to finding Coleman's hideout. Rosaria could at least point him in the right direction.

"I'll think about it," he said grudgingly. "For now...your ma won't even let you spend the night here?"

Rosaria turned back to her mother and again the rapid Spanish flew back and forth, accompanied by stern shakes of the older woman's head. Braddock didn't need a translation to know what her answer was.

"All right," he said with a disgusted scowl on his face. "Is there a place in town where we can get a room for the night?"

"The cantina. Santo may think I want to come back to work for him, though."

"Well, we'll set him straight about that in a hurry," Braddock snapped.

Rosaria took hold of her horse's reins and swung up into the saddle again. She said, "*Gracias*, G.W."

"It's Braddock. Braddock the bastard, remember?"

"Ah, sí," she said softly. "Such a bastard you are."

ROSARIA'S PREDICTION turned out to be correct. The man who owned the cantina welcomed her with open arms and said that his customers would be very happy to see that she had returned. Then he told her to go to his room in the back and wait for him.

That was when Braddock came in after tying the horses to the hitch rack outside, and Santo muttered something about "*Diablo Tejano*" and scurried back behind the bar. Braddock knew the man had seen the badge pinned to his shirt.

He took a silver dollar from his pocket and tossed it to Santo. To Rosario, he said, "Tell him that'll pay for our room tonight and also for someone to take care of our horses. And all our gear had better be there in the morning, too."

She smiled and repeated his instructions in Spanish. Santo nodded eagerly. Braddock didn't know if his eagerness came from fear or greed or both and supposed it didn't really matter.

The room was small, with space only for a single narrow bed, a table with a basin of water and a candle on it, and a chair. Braddock thought maybe he could sleep on the floor.

For now, he was more interested in the meal of tortillas, beans, chilies, and goat stew that Santo dished up. He'd had a lot of skimpy suppers on the trail in recent weeks and the food here was good, at least.

It was too bad for Santo, though, that the cantina didn't have any other customers tonight. When Braddock asked Rosaria about that, she said, "It is because word has gotten around that a Texas Ranger is here. My people fear the Rangers because of all the violence in the past."

"The Rangers never hurt any Mexicans except bandits who had it coming," Braddock said.

"That is the way you see it. The friends and families of those so-called bandits may have different opinions."

Braddock grunted. "It's not a matter of opinion. You raid across the border into Texas, you've got to expect the Rangers to come after you."

Rosaria didn't argue with that and they let the matter drop. Braddock didn't care for the feelings that went through him, though, when he thought about how these people hated and feared him. That just didn't seem right.

When they went back to their room, he lit the candle and then pulled the blanket off the bed and started to spread it on the floor.

"What are you doing?" Rosaria asked.

"I'll sleep down here. You can have the bed."

"Don't be a fool. We will share the bed."

Braddock started to shake his head but she went on, "You cannot still be afraid of me, G.W. You know I no longer have any place here. The only thing I can do is go with you. Why would I hurt you?"

"You *did* try to put a knife in my back," Braddock pointed out.

"Once! And that was days ago!"

He laughed. He supposed she was right.

She moved closer to him and lifted a hand to rest it on his beard-stubbled jaw. "We are much alike, you and I," she said.

"How do you figure that?"

"Fate has us in its grip and all we can do is let it carry us along."

"A man makes his own fate," Braddock growled.

"Do you honestly believe that? You said just the opposite before."

Braddock's head was whirling. He didn't know what he believed anymore and that came as a shock. He had always been so certain that life had one thing and one thing only in store for him: being a Texas Ranger. He had held tight to that, even when everybody seemed determined to rip it away from him. Now he just didn't know anymore...

He put his hand under Rosaria's chin and tipped her head up. "I only believe one thing tonight," he told her. "I believe I'll get in that bed with you."

13

———

BRADDOCK WOKE AND STRETCHED ON ROUGH SHEETS without opening his eyes. As he lay there he thought about the night just past, and as he did he realized with a shock that for the first time in ages, dreams had not haunted his sleep. At least, not any that he remembered. That was a blessing.

He didn't know if that peaceful slumber was because of Rosaria, but he didn't know who else to credit for it. He wondered where she was. He felt around in the bed to be sure that she wasn't there next to him.

Warm light shone against his closed eyelids. The sun was up and spilling through the room's lone window. Maybe Rosaria had gone out to get something for him to eat or some coffee. Not that he expected her to act like his servant. He didn't want that.

Gradually, he became aware that something besides the morning sunlight was coming in through the window. He heard sounds as well: the tramp of many feet, the clinking of harness, the mutter of voices. All that taken together set off alarm bells in Braddock's brain and his eyes popped open at last.

Braddock had placed his holstered Colt and coiled shell belt on the little table beside the bed so it would be handy. As he bolted upright he reached out and closed his hand around the revolver's grips. Footsteps sounded just outside the door. He jerked the gun from the holster and swung it in that direction.

His finger froze on the trigger as Rosaria flung the door open and hurried into the room. "Braddock!" she exclaimed as she stopped short and stared down the barrel of the gun.

"Damn it!" Braddock had already cocked the Colt. He pointed it at the plaster ceiling and lowered the hammer. "I almost shot you. What's going on out there?"

Rosaria was breathing hard. "Rurales," she said.

Braddock relaxed slightly. The Rurales were Mexico's frontier police force and this was probably just a routine patrol on its way through the village. He knew they had a reputation for corruption and brutality but at the same time they were lawmen like he was, and he hadn't done anything wrong by being here in Esperanza. True, he had ridden in wearing a Texas Ranger's badge and, as Rosaria had pointed out, the Rangers weren't well liked here but he hadn't shot anyone or tried to make any arrests.

"Don't worry," he told her. "They won't have any interest in us. We'll just wait until they leave—"

"You fool!" Rosaria broke in. "I was at the well when I saw Santo running to talk to them. He's bound to be telling them that a *Diablo Tejano* is in his cantina. *Presidente* Diaz hates Texans and Rangers in particular. The

Rurale commandant can gain favor with him by arresting you for being across the border without permission!"

Maybe she had a point there, Braddock thought. More than likely it would be better if he didn't fall into the hands of the Rurales. He slid the Colt back in its holster and stood up to reach for his clothes.

"I'll try to get to the horses and make a run for the border," he said. "If I can get on the other side of the river—"

A shout from outside interrupted him. "Ranger!" a harsh voice bellowed. "Ranger, I know you are in there! Come out with your hands in the air!"

Rosaria clenched her hands and looked terrified. "Too late," she said in a half-whisper.

Braddock stepped to the window and glanced out. He was surprised to discover that evidently the cantina was surrounded already. He could see several men in gray trousers and jackets and matching steeple-crowned sombreros. They wore holstered pistols and carried rifles and looked quite formidable.

If he tried to shoot his way out of here, Braddock thought, he wouldn't make it ten feet before they blew him to pieces.

He had a hollow feeling inside but he had faced plenty of trouble before and was still here, so he wasn't going to panic. He told Rosaria, "Look, I'll talk to their captain. Maybe I can reason with him. Texas is only a quarter of a mile away, for God's sake!"

"It won't matter," she said as she shook her head. "This is Mexico. And you are a Texas Ranger."

He supposed he should have thought of that before he agreed to bring her here, he told himself. At the very least he should have taken off his badge and pretended to be just a drifter. But it was too late for that now, so he would just have to deal with things as they were.

"You stay in here," he told Rosaria as he pulled his clothes on. "There's no need for you to get involved in this trouble. It's between me and the Rurales."

"I'm the reason you're here."

"Not really," Braddock said. He buckled on his gunbelt. "Tull Coleman's the reason I'm here. All of it comes back to him. Hawley, the Dutchman, all of it." He picked up his hat and put it on, then said again, "Stay here."

"Braddock—" She clutched at his arm as he started past her. He paused and looked down at her and she put her arms around his neck, pulled his head down and kissed him with the sort of fierce hunger that a whore wasn't supposed to feel. As she broke the kiss, she whispered, "I'm sorry."

"It'll be all right," he said. He wasn't sure he believed it anymore but he said it anyway.

He walked through the empty cantina. The man in charge of the Rurale patrol was still out front, shouting and demanding that the Ranger surrender. He abruptly fell silent as Braddock stepped through the open doorway.

"Buenos dias," Braddock said with a nod as he confronted the man, who wore the same sort of gray woolen uniform as the other Rurales, only with a few more decorations such as a red sash tied around his waist. He also wore a sheathed sword as well as a revolver. Braddock made a guess as to the man's rank and went on, "What can I do for you, *Capitan*?"

The officer was short and stocky and, like most of

his men, sported a thick, dark mustache. He glared at Braddock and said, "You are a Texas Ranger."

Braddock glanced down at his badge, smiled faintly, and nodded. "That's right. Ranger G.W. Braddock, at your service."

"I am *Capitan* Emiliano Mata, and you are not at my service, señor. You are my prisoner."

Braddock kept a carefully neutral expression on his face and in his voice as he asked, "Now why would you be arresting me, Captain? I haven't done anything wrong. I haven't broken any Mexican laws."

"You are an American in Mexico without official permission."

"How do you know I don't have your government's permission to be here?"

Mata's face flushed angrily. "I am in charge of this area. I would have been told."

"Well...folks from both sides go back and forth across the border all the time, I suspect, and nobody thinks much about it."

"Not Texas Rangers. Many times in the past the Rangers have come across the Rio Grande and attacked the Mexican people illegally and for no reason."

Braddock had heard about some of those border skirmishes and he didn't view them the same way Mata did. Right now, however, that didn't matter. Outnumbered the way he was, arguing about the history between their two countries would just antagonize the Rurale captain and make the situation worse.

"I give you my word, Captain, I mean no harm to your people. In fact, I was about to leave Esperanza and head back across the river to Texas. If you'll just let me get my horse, I'll move along, and this little incident will all be over."

If by some chance Mata let him go, he could always wait on the other side of the Rio Grande until the Rurale patrol had left the village, then come back across and get Rosaria. By now, he had accepted the idea that she would come with him, although he didn't know what he would do with her in the long run.

Captain Mata laughed but it wasn't a pleasant sound. "This incident, as you call it, will not be over until you have been dealt with by Mexican law. I hereby place you in custody. You will be sent to Mexico City and given a trial." He paused. "Then you will be sent to prison, probably for the rest of your life."

"Because I was a stone's throw on the wrong side of the river?"

"Because you are a damned Texas Ranger," Mata said as his face twisted with hatred.

That hollow feeling inside Braddock had grown until it just about filled him. He knew now there was no way out of this. He was vastly outnumbered and Mata was determined to impress his superiors by arresting a Texas Ranger.

He didn't suppose it would do any good to tell Mata that he wasn't really—

Braddock's jaw tightened as he cut that thought short. He *was* a Texas Ranger, no matter what anybody else said, and by God, he wasn't going to deny it just to try to save his own hide. The law was more important than that. The law was more important than anything, even his own life.

Especially his own life, because without the law it was nothing.

"Unbuckle your gunbelt, drop it, and step away from it," Mata ordered. He rested his hand on the butt of his own pistol.

"I don't reckon I can do that," Braddock said in a quiet but determined voice.

"Then my men will kill you."

Braddock had moved only a few feet beyond the doorway. He had a hunch that if he acted quickly enough, he could throw himself backward and get behind the protection of the thick adobe walls before the Rurales could shoot him.

But then they would just lay siege to the cantina and pour lead through every door and window and Rosaria was in there. The fate that awaited him was bad enough but it would be worse if he was responsible for her death. If he surrendered, the Rurales wouldn't have any reason to hurt her.

"All right, Captain," he said. "Tell your men not to get trigger-happy. I'm going to drop my gun."

"Carefully," Mata advised. "I would rather have a live Texas Ranger to send to Mexico City...but I suppose I could send your head if I have to."

Braddock unbuckled his gunbelt and lowered it to the ground. He stepped away from it and moved toward Mata with his hands held at shoulder height.

"Noooo!"

The scream came from inside the cantina. Braddock jerked around and saw Rosaria charge out into the open. She bent and scooped his Colt from its holster and, as she raised the gun, she cried, "Braddock, run!"

"Rosaria, no!" he shouted. He took a step toward her but it was too late. She had already thumbed back the hammer and flame spouted from the gun's muzzle.

The next instant, a thunderous roar like the world was ending filled the village as the Rurales opened fire. Horrified, Braddock saw a dozen crimson flowers bloom on Rosaria's white blouse as rifle slugs ripped through her body.

He twisted back toward Mata, determined to kill the captain with his bare hands before he died himself.

That wasn't fated to be, either. Mata had charged at him and was practically on top of him already. The Rurale officer had drawn his sword and swung it in a vicious stroke at Braddock. The blade slammed into Braddock's head and drove him off his feet. Hot blood sheeted down the side of his face as he fell. He saw it splatter redly in the dust around him.

The Rurales closed in. Booted feet crashed into his ribs. They struck him with rifle butts as well. The brutal torture went on for what seemed like hours before Mata's harsh voice forced the men back.

Standing over Braddock with the bloody sword still in his hand, Mata grinned down at him and said, "Do not think you will be lucky enough to die here, Ranger. You will live to see the inside of a prison cell. But, for now, look at the *puta* who tried to help you."

He pointed with the sword and Braddock seemed powerless not to turn his head and gaze across the dusty ground at Rosaria's body. She lay sprawled on her back with her head twisted toward him so that he could see her face, frozen in lines of agony, and her empty, staring eyes. He wished he could tell her how sorry he was but it was far too late for that.

Mata was still gloating but, somewhere along in there, Braddock passed out, so at least he didn't have to listen anymore.

14

COLEMAN KEPT HIS HORSE MOVING AT A FAST PACE AS HE headed for the border. He didn't want to run the animal to death but the rage he felt at Jeff Hawley's death made him less cautious than he might have been otherwise.

Not foolhardy, though. He didn't try to catch up all in one day. He stopped that night and let his mount rest for a few hours while he grabbed a little sleep himself. But he was up well before dawn, steering by the stars now. The tracks he'd been following headed due south, so he took a chance they continued that way. If he lost the trail, he'd backtrack and find it in the morning. But if his guess was right, he had made up some of the gap between himself and his quarry.

Prey might be a better word, he mused as he rode through the pre-dawn gloom. Because he sure as hell intended to kill whoever was responsible for Hawley's death, slowly and painfully if at all possible.

When the sky grew light enough for him to see, Coleman found the tracks very quickly, confirming that his hunch had been right. The three horses were still heading for the border. He rode on through the day, stopping only when he sensed that his horse was about to give out.

As long as this one got him where he was going, that was all he really cared about. He could put his hands on another saddle mount whenever he got there. After everything he had done in his life, he wouldn't hesitate to steal a horse.

He made camp for a while again that night, then pushed on. At mid-morning, he reached the Rio Grande. He could see the crude adobe structures of a Mexican village not far away on the other side of the river.

Had it been bandits from south of the border who killed Hawley and burned down Dutchman's Folly? That seemed possible to Coleman although, as far as he knew, there hadn't been much raiding along the border recently.

There was only one way to find out. The river was low enough here to ford, so Coleman sent his exhausted mount plodding through the water.

He noticed right away that quite a few horses were tied at the hitch racks in front of a building marked simply CANTINA, painted in somewhat shaky letters on the adobe above the arched entrance. Coleman counted eighteen saddled animals. Several men in gray clothes and sombreros lounged around the place, some of them hunkered on their heels in the shade cast by the walls, smoking short brown cigarettes, talking and laughing among themselves.

Coleman saw a few of the villagers moving around, too, going back and forth from the well by the church or visiting the settlement's one store. They avoided the sombreroed men.

Coleman had never encountered Rurales before but he had a pretty good hunch that was who these men were. Any sort of authority rubbed him the wrong way. The sight of the Rurales made him want to turn around and get the hell back over the border.

The tracks had led across the river and into this village, though. The men he was looking for were here and Coleman didn't intend to leave without them.

The Rurales paid no attention to him as he rode up to the store and dismounted. He would have preferred going into the cantina—it was always easier to pick up information in a place where men were drinking—but he didn't want to risk it. Maybe he could find out what he needed to know in here.

The inside of the place was cool and shadowy, full of the smells of coffee and peppers and spices. Coleman didn't see any customers but a squat, bald man with a dirty apron over his clothes stood behind a counter in the back. A look of alarm appeared on his face as Coleman approached him.

Coleman put a friendly grin on his face and tipped his hat back. He could be plenty charming when he wanted to.

"Howdy, amigo," he said. "How are you today?"

"You are a Texan?" the storekeeper asked nervously.

"That's right. Is that a problem? I didn't think folks paid too much attention to the border around here."

"Today is not a good day to be in Esperanza," the man said. "The Rurales have captured a Texas Ranger who had no right to be here. You...you are not one of those devils, are you, señor?"

"Me?" Coleman said. "Do I look like a Texas Ranger?"

"You don't look that much different from the man who was captured by *Capitan* Mata. You are the same sort, I think."

The storekeeper turned his head and glanced toward a barred door behind him. Coleman wasn't sure why he did that but the gesture seemed to have some meaning.

"Now hold on a minute," Coleman said. "I'm not sure I take kindly to being told I remind somebody of a Texas Ranger. I've had my own run-ins with those boys. What happened to this one?"

The storekeeper licked his lips and nodded toward the door. "He is locked up back there in my storeroom. *El Capitan* told me that if anything happened to him, he would have my head. And I believe *Capitan* Mata. He is a very hard man. You don't want him to find you on this side of the border, señor. Please, if you need supplies, tell me what they are. I will gather them and then you should get back across the border as quickly as you can!"

"Tell me more about that Ranger," Coleman insisted. Something stirred in the back of his mind, something he couldn't quite bring himself to believe but he wanted to hear more with his own ears.

"He is tall and lean. Like you. His hair is brown without the red in it like you have. And he has a mustache."

That sounded like...No, it couldn't be, Coleman thought.

The storekeeper went on, "When he was talking to *Capitan* Mata, he said his name was...Braddock, I think."

Coleman stood there like he'd been punched in the gut. He had trouble getting his breath for a moment. His pulse hammered in his head. When the reaction settled down, he said to the storekeeper in a flinty voice, "Tell me what happened here. Tell me all of it."

That didn't take long. When the storekeeper was finished with the tale, Coleman was convinced it really had been none other than G.W. Braddock who had ridden into Esperanza with one of the village girls who had gone off to be a whore in Texas. The girl was dead now and Braddock, wounded by the Rurale captain, was locked up only a few yards away. Coleman trembled with the desire to stalk over there, open the door, and empty his Colt into Braddock.

There were a couple of reasons why he didn't do that. One was the knowledge that the shots would bring the Rurales on the run and, in all likelihood, he would never leave this village alive.

The other was curiosity. Coleman knew good and well that Braddock wasn't a Texas Ranger anymore. Why was this Captain Mata so sure he was? Coleman wanted an answer to that riddle.

He also wanted to get Braddock out of here and back across the border, so he could deal with the bastard in his own time and on his own terms. But again, if he tried to bust Braddock out of captivity, the Rurales would kill him. The odds were just too high.

But Frank Wiley and the rest of the gang were on their way here, Coleman thought with a smile.

And when they arrived, the odds would be totally different.

A GROAN WELLED up from somewhere deep inside Braddock. Part of it was due to the terrible pain that filled his head but mostly it was composed of despair and sorrow. As soon as he'd returned from the welcome oblivion of unconsciousness, he had remembered how Rosaria died.

He hadn't cried over his ma's death or his pa's. He hadn't shed tears like that since he'd buried his dog. His father had driven that out of him. So his eyes remained dry now. He wasn't going to cry over a whore, even one he had come to like a little. But she had died trying to help him, so inside he mourned.

A little scurrying noise made him lift his head and open his eyes. He was in a small room somewhere with adobe walls, a hard-packed dirt floor, and a thatched roof with enough gaps in it to let in several shafts of sunlight. Burlap sacks of grain were stacked against one of the walls. A rat perched atop one of the sacks it had evidently just torn open. Its beady eyes stared at Braddock for a second, then it darted away, disappearing through the rip in the sack.

"Eat yourself to death, you furry little bastard," Braddock rasped. His voice sounded foreign to his ears.

He sat up, which made the storage room that was his makeshift prison spin crazily around him for a moment. He lifted a hand to his head where it throbbed the worst and his fingers touched cloth. A quick exploration told him that a rag of some sort had been tied around his head to serve as a bandage over the gash Captain Mata's sword had opened up. The cloth was crusty with dried blood. Braddock knew he had been unconscious for quite a while.

When his head settled down he looked around and

tried to figure out if there was any way out of here. He assumed the heavy wooden door was barred on the other side and there might even be a Rurale standing guard out there, too. The storeroom didn't have any windows. He might be able to tear a big enough hole in the roof to climb out...if he could stack up those grain sacks high enough to reach it.

But even if he succeeded in doing that, Mata's whole patrol was probably still in the village. He'd have to get through them and then make a dash for the river, more than likely on foot.

The odds of him getting away were so slim as to be non-existent.

But at least if he tried to escape, he could force them to kill him quickly, rather than having to endure a years-long death in captivity in some hellhole of a Mexico City prison. That was what he was going to do, Braddock decided. He would go out fast and if he could get his hands on a gun before he died, he would take some of the brutal sons of bitches with him.

He tried to stand up. That was a bigger job than it sounded like. Every muscle in his body was stiff and sore from the beating the Rurales had given him. He had to rest both hands on the rough wall and lean against it to steady himself as he climbed slowly, inch by inch, to his feet. By the time he was upright, he was covered with sweat and his chest heaved from the exertion.

Braddock sleeved some of the moisture off his face and waited until his heart stopped racing before he tried to move again. The room wasn't spinning around anymore, either. Carefully, he moved over to the sacks of grain and started rearranging them to form a slope he could climb to the roof.

He disturbed the rat, who burst out of one of the sacks and scurried into a corner. Braddock smiled grimly and said, "I know how you feel."

Then he heard voices on the other side of the door. His heart sank as the bar scraped in its brackets. That meant it was being taken down and the door was about to be opened. Braddock set himself and got ready to charge out as soon as he got a chance. He would go ahead and make them kill him right here and now.

The door swung back. Braddock lunged forward through the opening and, as he did, he spotted Captain Mata standing there with pistol in hand, pointing the weapon at him. Braddock's face twisted in a snarl as he braced himself for a bullet's impact.

Instead, something slammed into his back and knocked him down. Fresh bursts of pain exploded inside his head as he crashed to the floor. His muscles refused to work. Hate and rage could accomplish only so much.

Strong hands closed around his arms as two of the Rurales grabbed him and jerked him to his feet. Mata smirked at him and waved a finger back and forth.

"You don't get off that easy, Señor Ranger," he said. "Take him out and put him in the wagon."

This was the first Braddock had heard about a wagon. He wasn't surprised, though. They would have had a harder time keeping him from escaping if he'd been on horseback. That was why he had commandeered a wagon to transport Tull Coleman and Jeff Hawley when he'd captured them. And, of course, Hawley had been in no shape to ride, what with Braddock's bullet in his back...

The men holding Braddock marched him out

through the store and into the street. The Rurale troop was gathered there, most of them already mounted. A couple of men were seated on the driver's box of a wagon with its tailgate down. Another man waited in the back of that wagon with a length of chain in his hands. The chain had a shackle at each end.

Braddock saw the steel ring mounted in the middle of the wagon bed and knew they were going to chain him to it. This was his last chance, he thought desperately. Once he was shackled like that, he'd never get a chance to fight back. They would be able to take him wherever they wanted and do anything they pleased to him.

His captors lifted him, flung him into the wagon. He lay there with his brains screaming commands at his muscles. *Fight! Fight, damn you!*

The Rurale with the chain grinned down at him and said something in Spanish. Braddock was too stunned to follow the words very well but he understood just enough to know that the man was taunting him, daring him to fight, making fun of him for being a Texan...

Braddock was trying to summon the strength to get up off the wagon bed and throw a punch, just one punch, when a shot blasted and the head of the Rurale looming over him exploded like an overripe pumpkin.

15

THE RURALES WEREN'T EXPECTING ANY TROUBLE. THAT was obvious from the way they stood around gaping for several seconds while more shots rang out and half a dozen of them fell to the onslaught of lead.

The man who'd been about to shackle Braddock to the wagon dropped the chain as he died. Braddock grabbed the chain out of mid-air and it was as if the links served as a conduit for strength to pour into him from somewhere. He surged up in the wagon bed and lunged at the two men on the seat as they tried to turn around toward him. One of them clawed at the revolver on his hip.

Braddock slashed the heavy chain across the man's head. The sombrero absorbed some of the blow's force, but it was still enough to knock the man sprawling onto the horses hitched the wagon. Spooked, the animals let out shrill whinnies and charged forward.

Braddock almost went over backward as the wagon lurched into motion, but he caught his balance and backhanded the other Rurale with the chain. This time he caught the man on the jaw, which crunched and shattered under the impact. The Rurale slumped to the floorboard, groaning thickly as blood welled from his mouth.

The wagon swayed back and forth as it raced along the street toward the church. Braddock held the chain in his right hand and used the left to grab the back of the seat and brace himself. As he passed the jacals, he caught glimpses of men using the huts for cover as they continued their attack on the Rurales. Rifles spat fire and lead and more of the Mexican lawmen fell.

For a second, Braddock thought that the peasants who lived here had risen against the brutal authorities but he saw that wasn't the case. His rescuers were gringos like himself and his heart leaped as he wondered if the Texas Rangers had discovered somehow that he was a prisoner and had come to rescue him.

Then he spotted Captain Emiliano Mata and forgot all about such speculation for the moment. The officer was running toward the church, the same direction the runaway wagon was going. Maybe he intended to seek shelter there. Braddock didn't care. The wagon was about to overtake Mata, and as it did Braddock put a booted foot on the sideboards, levered himself up, and launched himself in a diving tackle.

He crashed into Mata from behind and drove him to the ground. The shock sent jolts of pain through Braddock's head and he felt fresh blood running down his face from the sword wound. He ignored that and scrambled after the chain he had dropped as Mata rolled over and tried to get his pistol out. The gun cleared leather just as Braddock grabbed the chain and swung it.

The chain slashed across the wrist of Mata's gun hand. He screamed as the revolver flew from his fingers. Braddock swung the chain back, aiming at Mata's face, but the captain got his left arm up in time and the chain wrapped around it instead. He used that to jerk Braddock toward him and met the Texan with a vicious kick to the belly. Braddock gasped and doubled over but he didn't lose his grip on the chain. He shook it loose and struggled to his feet.

Mata came up, too, dragging his sword from its scabbard. He hacked frantically at Braddock who flung the chain up and blocked the blade with it. For a long moment, the desperate battle surged back and forth, Mata slashing and thrusting with the sword while Braddock used the chain to parry it.

Then the blade went *through* one of the links of the chain and Braddock was able to twist it out of Mata's hand. He tossed both chain and sword aside as Mata came at him, punching and kicking. It was a near-miracle that Braddock had been able to put up as much of a fight as he had, injured as he was, and now the fuel of hatred and desperation was running out. He had to give ground before Mata's ferocious attack. He tripped on something, lost his balance, and fell backward.

What he had tripped on was Mata's sword and, as the Rurale captain rushed in to try to capitalize on what he saw as a momentary advantage, Braddock scooped up the sword and thrust up and out with it. Mata couldn't stop in time. The blade went into his belly and sliced through his guts before scraping off his spine and then ripping out from his back. He shrieked and pawed at the sword but he couldn't pull it free. All he succeeded in doing was slicing open his fingers on its keen edge.

Braddock gave Mata a shove to the side. The captain collapsed, curling around the agony in his belly and dying in that position. His death wouldn't bring Rosaria back, so Braddock took no real satisfaction in it, but Mata had gotten what he deserved, anyway.

And this slaughter of Rurales would cause an unpleasant incident between the governments of the United States and Mexico, especially if Braddock's rescuers really were Texas Rangers. Politics was the least of Braddock's worries just now, however. He felt like he might pass out at any moment.

The shooting in Esperanza had just about died away. He turned slowly to gaze along the street. The men who had saved him from spending the rest of his life in a Mexican prison had emerged from cover now and were stalking among the bodies of the fallen Rurales, casually finishing off any of the Mexicans who were still alive. Braddock didn't recognize any of them but blood was dripping into his eyes, causing a red haze that made it difficult to see clearly. He tried to wipe some of the blood away as he stumbled toward the men.

"Thank you," he croaked as he approached several of them. "You...you saved my life."

The men turned toward him, and Braddock stopped like he had run into a wall.

Tull Coleman grinned at him and said, "Why, you're mighty welcome, Ranger Braddock. Couldn't have no dirty Mexicans killing you when I want to do it myself."

BRADDOCK WAS IN HELL. At least, it would do until the real thing came along.

His arms were stretched out to the sides and tied to the posts that held up the roof over the well. He had hung there all day as he watched Coleman and the other outlaws brutalize the villagers and loot the place of its meager valuables. Men who had tried to fight back against them had been gunned down ruthlessly. Braddock didn't want to think about what had happened—and was still happening—to the women and girls of the village.

And all of it because of some politicians and lawyers who had seen to it that a mad dog like Tull Coleman was turned loose on the world once again. Braddock wished they could see the results of their crusade to bring down the Rangers.

But there was more blame to go around. After having him strung up like this, Coleman had gloated about tracking him here from Dutchman's Folly and sneaking into the village with the rest of the gang. If Braddock hadn't been so determined to bring Coleman to justice, he wouldn't have found Jeff Hawley. If he hadn't gone to the road ranch, he wouldn't have met Rosaria. He never would have brought her here and Coleman and the rest of those crazed killers couldn't have followed them.

So in a way, Braddock's feverish brain concluded, *he* was partially responsible for opening the gates of hell on Esperanza.

Now, night was falling and the flames leaping up from several of the buildings that were on fire cast a red glow over the entire village. In that glare, Tull

Coleman swaggered toward Braddock, rifle in one hand and bottle of tequila in the other.

Coleman was a little drunk, Braddock saw as the outlaw came to a stop in front of him and swayed slightly. With a big grin on his face, Coleman waved the bottle toward the rest of the town and said, "What do you think, Ranger? How do you like what we've done here? I had to let my boys blow off a little steam after they came all this way to give me a hand. The place'll never forget our visit, that's for damned sure!"

Braddock didn't say anything. He didn't want to give Coleman the satisfaction.

Coleman lifted his Winchester and used the muzzle to prod the badge still pinned to Braddock's shirt. "I don't understand. I know damned well they booted you out of the Rangers. You got no right to wear that badge."

"I'll always have the right to wear that badge," Braddock growled.

Coleman shook his head. "Not according to the law. And you know what that means?" He cackled and poked Braddock with the rifle barrel again. "It means you're an outlaw just like me, Braddock! You're on the wrong side of the law now, too!"

Braddock knew he couldn't go on if he allowed himself to believe that. He couldn't accept it. He knew he had done the right thing by continuing to try to enforce the law, no matter what the damned lawyers and politicians said.

Of course, it didn't really matter now, he thought. He was already half-dead and Coleman would take care of the other half sooner or later...when he got tired of terrorizing the village and tormenting his prisoner.

"What happened to your head, anyway?" Coleman asked abruptly. "You look like some sort of damned pirate from a storybook with that bloody rag around your head."

"That Rurale captain hit me with his sword when they captured me."

"The one you gutted like a fish with his own sword? I liked that, Braddock. It was almost enough to make me like you. I got no use for these damned greasers."

"Raul Gomez rode with you," Braddock pointed out.

"That was different. He was one of us...until you killed him." Coleman grew more serious. "Yeah, you killed Gomez and the rest of my men, even Jeff. It just took you longer to catch up to him."

Braddock shook his head and said, "I didn't kill Hawley."

Coleman snorted. "You don't expect me to believe that, do you?"

"It's the truth. All I wanted from him was information about where I could find you."

"Jeff never would've betrayed me!"

"He didn't," Braddock admitted. "He set himself on fire. I reckon he was tired of living in that chair."

"Where you put him." Coleman's face twisted in a snarl and, for a second, Braddock thought the outlaw was going to lift the Winchester and blow his brains out. After everything he had witnessed today, all the death and tragedy and horror, Braddock would have almost welcomed that.

"You're a damned coward."

Braddock shook his head. The voice seemed to come from everywhere and nowhere.

"Nobody has to kill you. You're already dead inside."

"No!" The word tore Braddock's throat painfully as it came out.

Coleman took it the wrong way. He sneered again and said, "Don't worry, Braddock. I'm not going to kill you yet. It's gonna take you a long time to die..."

You've given up. That's something a real *Ranger would never do.*

Braddock jerked against the bonds holding him to the well as he tried to get away from the words lashing at him. "Get the hell away from me, old man!" he screamed.

"Old man, is it?" Coleman said. "I'm not that much older than you. And you never did tell me how come you're still wearing that badge."

How about it, boy? Why do you deserve to wear the badge?

Braddock's head had sagged forward in exhaustion. Now, he found the strength to lift it and gaze into Coleman's eyes as he said, "I wear it because I'm a Ranger. I'll always be a Ranger, no matter what anybody else says. Anybody!"

"You know what you are, Braddock?" Coleman laughed. "You're loco! Plumb out of your mind. That's what you are. I reckon when I do finally kill you, I'll be doing you a favor."

Braddock spit at the outlaw's feet.

Coleman stepped closer, swung the rifle up, and smashed the stock across Braddock's face. Braddock hung there, blood dripping from his mouth now as it continued to ooze from his head injury as well. Coleman put his face close to Braddock's and his lips drew back from his teeth as he said, "Come sun-up, everybody who's still alive in this rathole is gonna die, Braddock. You're going to watch it and you'll know that it's on your head, you crazy fool. You think about that tonight."

He turned and stalked away, and behind him, barely conscious, Braddock muttered, "I'm a Ranger...a Ranger..."

It seemed like he heard someone say, *"Maybe you are, at that,"* but he couldn't be sure.

16

BRADDOCK WAS IN AND OUT OF CONSCIOUSNESS AS THE long, hellish night dragged on. He was sure that he hallucinated some due to loss of blood, the punishment he had endured, and sheer exhaustion. That was why he had thought he heard his father talking to him, he told himself. Those words had been figments of his fevered imagination.

Because of that, when he felt something tugging at the bonds around his right wrist, he thought that wasn't real, either.

Finally, when the feeling persisted, he raised his head wearily and turned it to look in that direction. He was shocked to see a shadowy figure crouched behind the well, reaching up to saw at the rope around his wrist with a knife.

Most of the fires had died down by now, so the red glare didn't spread across the entire village anymore. Shadows cloaked this end of the street. Coleman had posted one of the outlaws to keep an eye on him but the man was leaning against a hitch rack, half asleep after hours of debauchery earlier. He didn't seem to notice whoever it was cutting Braddock loose.

The rope fell away but Braddock kept his arm raised in the same position. That wasn't easy—after so many hours like this his muscles wanted to just go limp—but he knew that too much movement *would* attract the guard's attention.

Just as the fires had died down, so had the shooting and shouting and screaming. A harsh laugh sounded here and there but, for the most part, the village was quiet now. Quiet enough for Braddock to hear the soft whisper of bare feet against the dirt as the shadowy figure moved around the well to the other side. A moment later, he felt his rescuer start to cut the rope on his left wrist.

Braddock was at a loss as to who would risk their life to help him. He had no friends in Esperanza. In fact, the villagers who were still alive had good reason to hate him for his part in what had happened here.

But whoever it was, he was grateful to them. He was going to have one more chance—his *last* chance, certainly—to go out fighting instead of submitting meekly to his fate.

The rope around his left wrist came loose. He was free. Outnumbered, unarmed, and half dead...but free.

"*Señor.*"

The whispered voice belonged to a woman but other than that Braddock didn't recognize anything about it.

"A gun there is...behind the well. Four bullets only...all I could find."

"*Gracias,*" Braddock whispered in return, then indulged his curiosity. "Who...are you?"

"Rosaria...*mi hija.*"

My daughter...It was Rosaria's mother who had freed him. The woman who had turned Rosaria away...but also the one person in Esperanza who probably had the most reason to hate him, for the part he had played in Rosaria's death.

"These hombres...*malo. Muy malo.*"

Nobody could argue with that. Tull Coleman and his gang were very bad, all right. The baddest of the bad, Braddock thought.

"You kill them?" the woman said.

"As many as I can," he promised.

"*Bueno.* And you will die, too, I think."

Braddock understood now. She hated all of them, all the gringos who had brought their private feud to this village and caused its ruin. She was unleashing Braddock on them so he could kill as many of the outlaws as possible before he died himself. From her standpoint, that was about all the revenge she could hope for.

He would do his best to deliver it for her. For the woman's sake...and for Rosaria's.

"Distract the guard for a second," he told her, not knowing if she understood that much English. "Give me a chance to get my hands on that gun."

She made no reply but he heard her feet shuffling as she retreated from the well. He waited and, a moment later, she came into view at the corner of his eye, walking toward the guard.

The man straightened from his casual pose when he saw her coming. She stopped when she was between him and Braddock and started haranguing him, waving her arms in the air as she ranted at him in Spanish.

"What the hell," the guard said. "I don't understand

what you're goin' on about, you Mex bitch. Why don't you just skedaddle?"

Rosaria's mother kept it up, and while she was doing that, Braddock lowered his arms and slipped around to the back of the well. He was unsteady and had to brace himself with one hand on the low stone wall around the well while he felt on the ground in the darkness for the gun the woman had said was there.

His fingers brushed the barrel and closed around it. He picked up the gun and transferred his grip to the butt. It was an old single-action Colt but, as long as it worked, that was all that mattered. Quickly, he checked the barrel to make sure sand hadn't fouled it and found it clean.

The revolver held four rounds, she had said. Well, he would just have to make them count.

He stepped out from behind the well. The guard finally noticed him, eyes growing big as he stared over the woman's shoulder. He must have figured out what she'd been doing because he jerked up the rifle he held and used it to batter her aside, shouting, "You damned bitch!"

Braddock had to use both hands to aim and fire the Colt but he squeezed off a shot before the guard could do anything else. Because of the uncertain light, he aimed for the biggest target, the man's torso. As the gun in Braddock's hand blasted, the guard staggered. Braddock knew he'd hit the man. But the guard wasn't down and he managed to fire the Winchester. The slug chewed splinters from one of the well posts next to Braddock.

Braddock had already thumbed back the hammer. He fired a second shot and this one knocked the guard over on his back. Braddock stumbled forward as he eared back the hammer again. The guard lay there gasping and arching his back like a fish that had been hauled out of a pond. He gave a gurgling groan and then sagged limply on the ground.

Braddock stuck the old revolver in the waistband of his trousers and bent to pick up the guard's fallen rifle and jerk the man's pistol from its holster. While he was doing that, the woman climbed back to her feet.

"Kill them all," she said.

"That's the general idea," Braddock said.

But it wouldn't be easy, the shape he was in, outnumbered as he was. The two shots hadn't drawn any attention so far. Shots had been ringing out all over the village all night as the outlaws wreaked their havoc. That respite wouldn't last, though. In a minute or so, somebody would realize they had heard both a rifle and a pistol and they would come to see what the exchange of shots had been about. Not everybody would be so sated by booze and violence that they couldn't think straight.

"You'd better get out of sight," Braddock went on. "*Gracias.*"

If he'd had any doubts about the way she felt toward him, the way she spat at his feet before she scurried off erased them. To her, he was just the lesser of two evils, a blunt instrument to be used against the men she despised even more.

That was all right with him. Carrying the weapons he had taken from the guard, he trotted off into the shadows.

Judging by the stars, it was a couple of hours until dawn and he had a lot of work to do in that time.

THE CANTINA HAD A BACK DOOR, Braddock recalled, so he circled toward it. Some of the outlaws were bound to be there and Coleman might be one of them.

While he wanted to kill as many of the gang as possible before they got him, his main goal was to put a bullet through Tull Coleman's brain. He didn't need some sort of dramatic showdown. If he had the chance to shoot Coleman in the head from behind, he would take it. All that mattered was putting him down like a hydrophobia skunk, so he couldn't spread any more of his evil through the world.

He eased the building's rear door open and slipped into the darkened hallway. Enough light came through the beaded curtain at the other end for him to see the door of the room where he had spent the night with Rosaria and that caused his guts to twist for a second. It was hard to believe that less than twenty-four hours ago, she had still been alive, snuggled warm and vital against him in the narrow bunk.

The room was occupied now. Braddock heard sobbing from inside, along with a man's harsh, panting breath. Moving soundlessly, he stepped through the door and let his eyes adjust to the darkness. He could make out the entwined shapes on the bed. He knew from the crying that it wasn't the girl's idea to be here.

Braddock moved closer to the bed and raised the rifle in both hands. He would have to strike swiftly and surely to avoid raising a commotion. When he was as sure of his target as he could be under these circumstances, he brought the Winchester's butt crashing down on the outlaw's head.

Bone shattered under the blow and the woman

screamed as the man collapsed on top of her. The scream wouldn't draw any attention from the other outlaws in the place, Braddock thought. At least he hoped it wouldn't.

He had put so much effort into the blow that he almost fell. He caught himself with one hand on the bed and then reached past the dead man to clamp that hand over the woman's mouth so she couldn't raise any more ruckus. He leaned close and whispered, "I'm a friend. Amigo. I won't hurt you. You understand?"

She nodded hesitantly, so Braddock risked lifting his hand. Other than breathing heavily, she didn't make a sound.

He grasped the dead man's shoulder and rolled him off the bed. The corpse thudded to the floor. The sound made Braddock wince but it couldn't be helped.

"You speak English? How many more of them are here?"

She understood enough to grasp the meaning of his question, although she answered in Spanish. "*Tres.*"

Her voice was young. How young, Braddock didn't want to think about. Instead, he whispered, "*Gracias.*"

The man's trousers were down around his ankles. It was a repulsive task but Braddock felt around until he located the man's holstered gun and also a sheathed knife. He unbuckled the belt and strapped it around his lean hips. He was turning into a walking armory, he thought as a faint smile tugged at his lips in the darkness. Now he had a rifle, three handguns, and a knife.

He would probably need all of them before the night was over.

"You run on home," he told the girl. She hurried

out, pulling a ripped dress around her as she headed toward the back door.

Braddock turned toward the front of the cantina.

The other rooms here in the back seemed to be empty and he saw why when he reached the curtain and peered through the screen of beads. The other three outlaws sat at a table, passing around a bottle of tequila. They had either already taken their turn with the girl or were waiting for it.

Braddock spotted Santo slumped forward over the bar. At first, he thought the proprietor was sleeping but then he saw the drops falling slowly from the puddle of blood that had reached the front edge of the bar. More than likely the outlaws had cut Santo's throat and he'd collapsed over the bar as he died. He was still balanced there.

None of the men at the table was Tull Coleman. But they were all killers, rapists, arsonists, and thieves, Braddock told himself. As a Texas Ranger, it was his job to bring them to justice. Here and now there was only one way to do that. The thought propped up his fading strength.

He hoped they were drunk enough that their reactions wouldn't be very fast. Right now, his sure weren't. His eyesight wasn't too clear, either. Luckily, the range was only a matter of a few yards.

He stepped through the curtains. The outlaws had to have heard the beads clicking together but they would think it was just their friend coming back from having his fun with that poor girl.

Braddock lined his sights on the back of the man closest to him and pulled the trigger. The Winchester cracked and blew the bastard's brains out. The outlaw fell forward across the table as blood, bone fragments, and gray matter sprayed in the faces of his companions.

They were shocked enough that Braddock was able to lever the rifle and shoot one of them in the chest before the third man finally reacted and surged up from his chair as he clawed out the gun on his hip. Braddock fired and turned the outlaw halfway around with the shot. He levered and squeezed off a fourth round. This one struck the last man in the jaw and tore it away, leaving him to make a strangled sound that tried to be a scream but couldn't quite make it. As he made a last-ditch attempt to lift his gun, Braddock shot him in the head and dropped him for good.

That flurry of shots, on top of the ones earlier, was bound to bring attention. Braddock lowered the rifle, wheeled around, and hurried out the back of the cantina. He heard men shouting in alarm somewhere along the street.

Any time now, somebody would notice that he was no longer tied to the well. They would figure out that he was the one stalking through the shadows and killing them.

He smiled bleakly as he imagined how well Tull Coleman would take *that* news.

"FIND HIM!" COLEMAN SCREECHED AS BLACK FURY threatened to consume him. "Find him and bring him to me!"

How the hell did Braddock do it? he asked himself as he stalked back and forth in front of the well where the former Texas Ranger was supposed to be tied. Braddock had been stripped of his badge and disgraced, yet he had come back from that to cause more trouble for Coleman. He had survived a run-in with the Rurales, including an ugly head wound from a saber, he'd had the hell beaten out of him several times, and he'd been strung up like a sack of meat.

And yet, Braddock was still alive and a handful of Coleman's men were dead, including the one who'd been guarding the former Texas Ranger.

The bastard had had help to escape. Coleman knew that because one of his men had brought a torch and they had found the pieces of rope that had been used to tie Braddock to the well. Those ropes had been cut. One of the villagers had dared to set him free. That surprised Coleman. He had believed that the survivors were thoroughly cowed.

He felt better than ever about his decision to kill everybody here and finish burning the place to the ground. They had it coming, the dirty greasers, he thought.

Some of his men had already started looking for Braddock but the others were just standing around looking confused. They'd had too much to drink, sated their appetites too much. They were groggy with their own decadence. Coleman waved an arm at them and yelled, "What the hell are you waiting for? Spread out and find that son of a bitch!"

The men began to disperse cautiously. Most had worried looks on their faces. Five of their pards had been struck down by an avenging force out of the shadows and it might come for *them* next. There was just no telling.

Shots blasted at the other end of town. "He's here!" one of the outlaws screamed. "He's—"

Braddock looped his arm around the man's neck, jerked his head back, and ripped the knife across the tight-drawn throat. Blood gushed blackly, fountaining out a good ten feet. Braddock let go of the outlaw and stepped back as the man dropped to the ground to gurgle out his last few breaths.

Two more members of the gang were lying in a tangled sprawl behind him where he had gunned them down. Neither had moved since they fell, so Braddock was confident they were either dead or dying. He left them there and trotted off into the deeper shadows.

He heard more of the outlaws coming but they weren't charging ahead blindly anymore. They were being careful now because he had managed to spook them which was exactly what he wanted.

A few minutes earlier, he had spotted Coleman at the other end of the street and seriously considered taking a shot at the boss outlaw. He'd decided against it because he was just too damned shaky. He wasn't sure he could hit the target at that range. When the time came for him to finish off Tull Coleman, he wanted to make sure of the kill.

On the other hand, he had to wonder how much longer he could continue like this. He was operating now on pure hate and that wouldn't keep him going forever. Sooner or later—probably sooner—his battered body would collapse and there would be nothing he could do to stop it.

Coleman had to be dead before that happened.

Braddock leaned against the rear wall of a burned-out hut and closed his eyes for a moment to gather what strength he had left. As he stood there, he heard rough voices approaching. He set the rifle against the wall and drew two of the revolvers.

One of the men coming around the hut said, "I'm thinkin' about saddlin' my horse and gettin' out of here. Seems to me this place must be cursed. How could it not be, with all the dyin' that's gone on since yesterday mornin'?"

"You try to leave now before we catch that damn Ranger and Tull's liable to shoot you himself. I never saw anybody with such a powerful hate for a fella."

"Tull says he ain't really a Ranger."

The other outlaw snorted and said, "He's wearin' that star in a circle and it appears he's pure hell on wheels when it comes to fightin'. That says Ranger to me, no matter what anybody else claims."

Even the shape he was in, that put a smile on Braddock's face for a second.

Then, as the men came around the corner of the building, he raised both guns, pointed them at the shadowy figures, and began thumbing off shots as fast as he could.

The slugs tore into the outlaws and made them jitter backward in a bizarre dance for a couple of steps before they collapsed. As they fell, Braddock pouched the iron in his right hand and grabbed the Winchester. He dashed across to another half-destroyed hut and clambered over a wall that had fallen in for the most part. He dropped to a knee, rested the rifle on what was left of the wall, and waited.

Three men ran up to the ones he had just shot. As they cursed in surprise at the discovery, Braddock opened fire again. He emptied the Winchester and dropped two of them, but the third man reached the corner of the hut and took cover there as he returned Braddock's fire. Braddock ducked as bullets smacked into the adobe wall near him.

More men shouted nearby and he heard running footsteps. They were closing in around him now. If he didn't get out, they would trap him here and he wouldn't get to kill Tull Coleman.

With that thought to spur him on, he waited for a lull in the firing from the other hut and then lurched to his feet, vaulted over the wall, and made a dash away from there. He left the rifle since it was empty and he didn't have any more ammunition for it.

A dark shape appeared in front of him. Colt flame bloomed in the predawn shadows. Braddock felt the wind-rip of a bullet past his ear as he triggered the Colt in his hand. The outlaw grunted and spun away.

He hadn't missed many shots tonight, Braddock thought as he kept running toward the old church. It was almost like some other agency was guiding his aim, another set of eyes and hands hovering behind him, directing his bullets.

But that was crazy.

Damned if he was going to give the old man credit for something like that.

A rifle spit fire at him from the right. He heard the whipcrack of the slug as it passed close by. Someone else opened up on him from the left. He was in a cross-fire and knew he stood little chance of making it to the church.

Then more shots sounded and a man cried out in pain. Both rifles bracketing him fell silent. Had the outlaws, inadvertently, shot each other? Braddock had no idea but he kept moving. He wasn't running now so much as stumbling but the church was right in front of him. He grabbed one of the double doors at the entrance, jerked it open, and half-ran, half-fell into the stygian darkness inside.

He bumped into something, felt of it and realized it was a pew. As he slid down onto it, he wondered if the priest was hiding out or had been killed by the outlaws. *La Catedral de la Esperanza*, Rosaria had called this place. The Cathedral of Hope. He'd been making a grim joke when he suggested maybe it should be called No Hope but that had turned out to be right.

As Braddock sat there trying to catch his breath, he heard more shots somewhere outside, followed by the swift rataplan of hoofbeats. Some of Coleman's men must have had enough and were taking off for the tall and uncut despite their fear of their leader. That would make the odds against Braddock a little better.

The shots, he decided, were just wild ones as the spooked outlaws blazed away at shadows.

The guns fell silent and the hoofbeats faded away. A hush settled over the village. Braddock didn't expect it to last for long and, sure enough, it didn't.

"Braddock!" That hoarse screech came from Tull Coleman. "Braddock, where are you? Come on out and face me, you son of a bitch! You goddamn phony Ranger!"

Those words made anger well up inside Braddock. Deep down, in his own heart, he still considered himself a Ranger and always would. To have scum of the earth like Tull Coleman accuse him of being a phony was more than Braddock could stand.

He pushed himself to his feet and started checking his guns. Two of the revolvers were empty and the other held only two rounds.

He had six more cartridges in the loops on the gunbelt, he discovered when he checked them. And they wouldn't fit the gun Rosaria's mother had given him. Braddock set it on the pew. He thumbed four cartridges into one of the remaining guns and the other two into the cylinder that was already partially loaded.

Eight rounds. They would have to be enough.

"Braddock!" Coleman screamed. He sounded a little closer now, like he was coming toward the church. "Braddock, where are you?"

For a long moment, Braddock stood there with his arms down at his sides, a gun in each hand. A bone-deep weariness stronger than anything he had ever experienced filled him. He had absorbed too much punishment over the past few days. Even more than that, he had seen too much death. His soul was awash in fire and blood. His hands would never be clean.

The only atonement he could make, and it was a slight one, was to see to it that Tull Coleman never hurt anybody else.

"Braddock!"

He strode to the church doors, kicked them open, and stepped out as his hands came up filled with the two guns.

"Right here, Coleman!" he cried.

The outlaw was twenty feet away. Braddock didn't see anything else moving on Esperanza's lone street. Coleman's gun was already drawn, too, and even though Braddock had a slight head start on him, Coleman was in better shape. His gun came level first and flame spouted from the muzzle.

Braddock felt the hammerblow of a slug against his chest and rocked back a step but he didn't fall. He brought both revolvers to bear on Coleman's chest and squeezed the triggers. The guns roared and bucked against his palms as he fired two shots from each of them.

Coleman jerked back, jolted by the bullets' impact. His gun hand sagged. His Colt blasted again but the bullet went into the dirt at his feet. His mouth opened, and he rasped, "You...damn...Ranger," before blood welled out over his chin. He pitched forward and landed on his face.

"You got that right," Braddock said.

His strength was finally gone, drained completely from him, and he felt like he might never get it back. The guns still held two bullets each but he couldn't hang on to them anymore. They slipped from his fingers and thudded to the ground in front of his feet.

He reeled backward and the only thing that stopped him from falling was that his back hit one of the church doors, which had rebounded shut after he kicked them open and stepped through. He leaned against it and waited for the rest of Coleman's men to kill him but nothing happened. The echoes of the shots rolled away and Esperanza was silent.

Braddock's legs wouldn't hold him up. He started to slide slowly down the church door until he was sitting in front of it with his legs stretched out in front of him. His head drooped and as he saw the dark bloodstain on his chest he realized the sky had gone gray with the approach of dawn.

There were worse places to sit and wait for death to claim him than the doorstep of a church, he thought. He'd never been a particularly religious man and, after everything that had happened, he figured God wouldn't want anything to do with him, if there was a God, but Braddock took comfort in where he had wound up, anyway.

He started to close his eyes but then something made him struggle to lift his head again. He looked along the street and saw a tall, imposing figure striding toward him through the gloom. Even though the sun wasn't up yet, the star on the man's chest seemed to glow with the reflection of the onrushing day. Braddock's lips were dry and cracked and his tongue was swollen but he forced himself to whisper, "Pa?"

The man kept coming, tall, so tall, with high-crowned hat on his head and duster sweeping around his legs and, now, there were two more men flanking him, just behind him. They looked much the same, all with badges on their vests, and Braddock realized they weren't ghosts or angels or even demons come to drag him down to hell.

They were Texas Rangers.

That was the last thing Braddock knew for a long time.

HE CAME TO HIS SENSES, NINE DAYS LATER, IN A ROOM at the mission with the brown-robed priest tending to him. Braddock figured the padre was going to give him the last rites but the mild-faced, balding man smiled and said in barely accented English, "You are well on your way to recovery, *Señor* Braddock."

"I'm not...gonna die?"

"We are all going to die sooner or later, *señor*. But my feeling is that *El Señor Dios* is not yet ready for you to depart this earth."

Braddock had a feeling *El Diablo* would be a lot more interested in his final whereabouts, but it seemed wrong to argue with a priest inside a church so he didn't say anything about that. Instead, he asked, "Is this Esperanza?"

"*Sí.*"

"What happened...after Coleman and I shot it out?"

"Three men brought you here and asked that I care for you. *Tejanos.* Rangers. Like you."

Not like him, Braddock started to say, then stopped

himself. Maybe it was because he'd been hurt so bad and had been unconscious, or at least out of his head for so long, but he was having a hard time wrapping his brain around what the priest had just told him.

"Rangers...here?" he asked.

The padre nodded. "One of them asked me to tell you that Captain Hughes sent them to find you. To...arrest you. But he said that since you were in Mexico, he and his friends had no jurisdiction, no right to take you in."

That legal nicety wouldn't stop most Rangers, Braddock knew, when they felt like they were in the right. He was certain of that because he had bent a few rules himself along the way. But being on the wrong side of the border...that made a good excuse when you didn't really want to carry out your orders. When you weren't sure you'd be doing the right thing if you did.

"They're the ones who helped me," he said in a half-whisper. "When I was fighting Coleman's gang. There really was somebody giving me a hand."

"*Sí, señor.* They trailed you here from a place called..." The priest sounded doubtful. "Dutchman's Folly?"

Braddock leaned back against the pillow behind him and said, "That's right." He could see now what had happened. Word of what had happened in Ozona had reached Captain Hughes and he'd dispatched a trio of Rangers to bring him in. As limited as the number of men at the captain's disposal was, Hughes must have really wanted him found. The trail had led from Ozona to Dutchman's Folly and then to Esperanza and the Rangers had arrived just in time to take a hand in the fight, borders be damned.

But then, instead of taking him in, they had left him and asked this priest to nurse him back to health.

He was curious about that but he wanted to know something else first. "The village," he said. "How bad...?"

"Very bad," the priest said with a solemn expression wreathing his face. "There are many new graves in the churchyard. But those who are left will go on. These are poor people, *señor*. They are accustomed to life handing them more than their share of bad fortune. Their reward will be in heaven, in the time to come someday."

Braddock hoped that was right, for the sake of the villagers of Esperanza. He said, "I'm surprised they don't hate me. I brought all this on them."

The padre shook his head. "No, *señor*. *Capitan* Mata and his Rurales were evil men. So were *Señor* Coleman and his men. You opposed them. This means you are a good man."

Braddock wished it were that simple. But again, he didn't want to argue with a priest...

"You said I was healing up."

"*Sí*. You needed rest more than anything else. And for the wound on your head to be cleaned and stitched. I'm afraid it will leave quite a scar. Your hair may never grow back there."

Braddock shook his head and said, "I don't care about that." He frowned. "I thought Coleman shot me in the chest."

"The bullet barely penetrated. I was able to dig it out. The wound was not a bad one."

That didn't make any sense, Braddock thought. But that was true about a lot of things in his life recently.

"What am I going to do now?" he mused, sighing as he looked out the window.

The priest hesitated. "The Ranger who asked me to care for you...he gave me a message and requested that I pass it along to you when you were in your right mind again."

Braddock wasn't sure that would ever be the case again but he looked at the priest with interest.

The man went on, "The Ranger declared that he would not arrest you because you were in Mexico, as I told you before, and also because you killed this bandit Tull Coleman, who was very bad and deserved to die. But he told me to make sure you understand...if you ever set foot across the border in Texas again, the Rangers will be waiting for you. He said you should stay in Mexico if you know what is good for you."

"I can't do my job in Mexico," Braddock growled. "As soon as I'm on my feet again, I'll need to get back to my work."

"I am just telling you what he said, *señor*," the priest said with a shrug and a smile. He started to turn away. "Now I should bring you some soup. You must get your strength back and that will help." He paused at a little table beside the door. "Oh, yes. The Ranger said you would want this. Actually, he said he was *afraid* you would want this."

Braddock held out his hand and the brown-robed man dropped something on his palm. As Braddock stared down at the object, he felt a chill go through him. Now he knew why Coleman's bullet hadn't penetrated deep enough into his chest to kill him.

What he held in his hand was his Texas Ranger badge with a bullet hole punched neatly in the center of the silver star.

HANGMAN'S KNOT

1

BREWSTER COUNTY, TEXAS, 1900

THE FIRST WARNING THE PEOPLE OF SANTA ANGELINA
had was a rumble like distant thunder. The sky that
morning was a clear blue with no storm clouds
anywhere in sight. Rain was unusual here in arid West
Texas, anyway. People looked around, frowned,
muttered.

Then somebody noticed the dust cloud rising just
outside the town and let out a shout. No one knew
what was coming but there was an immediate sense
that it couldn't be anything good. Women grabbed kids
and hurried to get off the street. Men jerked their
heads from side to side as they looked around, trying
to figure out what to do.

Less than a minute later, the twenty riders swept
into town, yelling and shooting. One of the townsmen
caught out in the open screamed and arched his back
as a bullet struck him from behind, shattering his
spine and bursting out through his guts. He stumbled a

145

couple more steps as blood poured from the exit wound and then pitched forward on his face.

Another man, a rancher who had come into town to pick up some supplies, crouched behind his wagon and aimed his single-shot rifle at the attacking horsemen. He fired, but with all the dust swirling around he couldn't tell if he hit any of the invaders. He bent forward as he fumbled to reload and, because of that, the slug that found him went through the crown of his hat, hit the top of his head, and bored on into his brain, killing him instantly.

Along both sides of the street, more men died, cut down by the hail of lead that swept the boardwalks and the front of the buildings. One slow-footed hombre was trampled to bloody hash by the steel-shod hooves of the horses as he tried to flee. The shooting didn't stop until the riders reached the far end of the street.

There they regrouped and reloaded and then they charged back through town and continued the slaughter.

Inside the Santa Angelina marshal's office, Deputy Tom Nation finished thumbing cartridges into the Winchester he held. The hammering of the pulse in his head seemed almost as loud as the shooting outside. He'd been dozing on the cot in the back room when the attack started, and by the time he'd jumped up, shoved his feet into his boots, run in here and grabbed the rifle and started loading it, the horsebackers had reached the end of the street, turned around, and started unleashing chaos again. Tom didn't know where Marshal Whitby was but he knew his duty.

He had to get out there and protect the town.

All he had to do was get his leg muscles to work. At

the moment, they seemed to be frozen solid.

"Damn it!" Tom said. He worked the rifle's lever to throw a shell into the chamber. The curse and the metallic sound of the Winchester's action broke through the fear that gripped him. He forced himself to move. He ran to the door and jerked it open just as the killers swept past again.

A bullet hit the door jamb and threw splinters from it. Tom flinched but he brought the rifle to his shoulder and pulled the trigger. The Winchester cracked and kicked. One of the riders toppled from the saddle.

That drew the attention of two of the attackers. They whirled their horses toward the marshal's office and blasted shots at the open door. Tom dived to the side and grunted as he landed hard on the floor. He got his knees under him and scrambled toward one of the windows, where he stood up, threw the shutters open, and thrust the rifle out. The two outlaws were charging toward the office as if they intended to ride right through the door.

Tom fired five shots as fast as he could work the Winchester's lever. One of the men rocked back in his saddle as a bullet caught him in the chest. The other man's horse screamed and stumbled and went down, mortally wounded. The other horse ran into it, tripped, and fell, too. Dust hid the tangle of men and flailing horseflesh.

Breathing hard, Tom ran out the back door, turned and pounded along the alley behind the buildings. He cut into one of the narrow passages leading to the street. When he reached the front corner, he saw that he was between Donegan's Hardware and the drugstore.

Some of the outlaws were swarming toward the bank. These men who had invaded Santa Angelina on a hot, sleepy morning were interested in more than death and destruction.

The others were just about back to the north end of town, where they had started spreading carnage mere minutes earlier. It seemed to Tom that the attack had been going on for half an hour, anyway, but he knew that wasn't right.

He leaned against the hardware store's front wall and aimed after the horsemen. He hoped they would just keep riding this time instead of turning around for another savage pass through the town. Maybe a shot or two would help speed them on their way.

Tom squeezed the trigger, worked the lever, fired again. He couldn't tell if he hit any of the raiders.

They didn't leave, though. They turned their horses around yet again and spurred the animals forward.

This time, however, instead of shooting they threw things at the buildings they passed. Tom's eyes stung and watered so much from the dust hanging in the air that, at first, he couldn't see well enough to understand what they were doing.

Then the first giant ball of flame blossomed and he knew. They were throwing crude bombs, bottles of kerosene with burning rags stuffed in the necks. When those bottles broke, the kerosene sprayed out and ignited, spreading fire along the boardwalks and the buildings.

Tom didn't know if his eyes were still watering from the dust or if he was crying from rage and frustration. Half a dozen fires were already burning and he knew he couldn't do anything to stop the town from becoming an inferno. With an incoherent shout, he started shooting again, emptying the Winchester this time. The riders galloped on past and continued to spread their hellfire.

Tom threw the empty Winchester aside. He had a Colt holstered on his hip, so he pulled that as he ran out into the street. It was clear now that the invaders intended to kill everybody in Santa Angelina, so the only thing he could do was go out fighting. He would meet them standing on his feet, shooting until the revolver was empty, and then they would ride him down.

Clouds of black smoke rolled from the burning buildings and mixed with the dust to form a blinding blanket. Tom couldn't see very far through it, but he heard more screams and shots. He imagined the attackers were cutting down more townspeople as the flames forced them to run out into the open.

"Come on, you sons of bitches!" he yelled. "Come on!"

A man on foot lunged out of the smoke at him. Tom caught a glimpse of the blood on the man's shirt and knew that he was wounded. He stepped forward, intending to help the man, but then the man tackled him instead, knocking the gun out of his hand and driving him over backward.

The man's weight landed on top of him and drove the breath out of Tom's body. The back of his head hit the ground hard enough to stun him. Tom's senses swam crazily. Then he regained enough of his wits to realize that the man's hands were around his neck, choking him.

Tom flailed and bucked but he couldn't get rid of the weight on his chest or the iron bands around his neck. The fingers of his right hand brushed against something, recognized it as the barrel of the Colt he had dropped. He closed his hand around the barrel and brought the gun up to crash it as hard as he could against the man's head.

That did the trick. The man let go of Tom's throat and slumped to the side. Tom fought his way out from under the senseless body, gasping for breath as he did so. Instead of clean air, though, he got a lungful of smoke and dust that sent wracking coughs through his body.

If he stayed here he would die from the smoke, even if the flames didn't get him. He staggered to his feet and was about to stumble away when he hesitated and looked down at the man he had clouted.

Tom didn't know if the man was a citizen of Santa Angelina or one of the invaders. The man's face wasn't familiar, at least what Tom could see of it through his tear-streaming eyes, but that didn't mean anything. He didn't know everybody in town. For that matter, the man could be a cowboy who rode for one of the spreads scattered along the Rio Grande, a few miles south of here. Tom sure wasn't acquainted with all of those punchers.

He shoved his Colt back in its holster, bent down, grabbed the unconscious man under the arms, and started dragging him toward the alley. Sure, the fella had tried to strangle him, but that could have been because he was crazed from his wound and all the chaos around him. Anybody could panic and lash out in dire circumstances like that.

Tom might not be able to save anybody else but he could save himself and this hombre, he told himself. They had to get clear of the fire.

For a few moments, Tom's world consisted entirely

of smoke and flame and fear. He was lean and wiry, not the strongest fella around, and dragging the man was difficult. The easiest thing would have been to lie down and give up but he forced himself to keep moving, backing through the smoke as he dragged the unconscious man.

Then he burst out into clearer air and it was like nectar as it poured into his tortured lungs. He wasn't safe, though, and he knew it. He needed to put more distance between himself and the conflagration. So he kept moving stubbornly away from the inferno that had been Santa Angelina.

He didn't stop until he stepped back into empty air and fell into a dry wash about a hundred yards from the edge of town. The man he had brought with him tumbled down the slope with him.

Tom sprawled face down on the sandy bed of the wash. He pushed himself up, shook his head, and looked around. The man lay a few feet away, still out cold, with his face turned toward Tom.

The deputy blinked, pawed at his eyes with the back of his hand. Away from the smoke and the dust, his vision began to clear, and he got his first good look at the man who had jumped him. A shock of recognition went through Tom.

He was looking at Henry Pollard, whose brother Amos owned one of the biggest ranches between El Paso and Del Rio.

Nobody in Santa Angelina had seen Henry Pollard in the past six months. The rumor was that his brother Amos had sent him to San Antonio or Austin or Fort Worth, somewhere well away from the border country after the terrible incident with June Castle.

Now, it appeared that he had come back to Santa

Angelina—and brought hell with him.

Because Tom was convinced Henry Pollard was the raider he had knocked out of the saddle with his first shot.

Tom drew his gun, which somehow had stayed in its holster during that tumble into the wash. If Henry was loco enough to be part of that raid, Tom didn't want to be unarmed around him. Henry's holster was empty but he was still dangerous.

Even down here in the bottom of the wash, the huge column of black smoke rising from the burning town was visible, filling a large swath of the sky. Still gripping his Colt, Tom climbed to the top of the slope.

The whole settlement was ablaze, just as he feared. He didn't hear any more shooting, though, so he hoped the raiders had gone, leaving their devastation behind them. Some of the townspeople might escape with their lives, even though everything else they possessed was destroyed.

He heard a groan from the bottom of the wash. When he looked around, he saw Henry Pollard stirring. Tom slid back down. Pollard wasn't fully conscious yet, but his eyes fluttered open as Tom rolled him onto his back.

Tom stood over him, pointing Pollard's own gun down at him. The deputy grimaced as he said, "I ought to go ahead and shoot you like the mad dog you are, Henry. You're responsible for this, damn you! I know you are!" With an effort, Tom brought his raging emotions under control and went on, "You don't look like you're hurt too bad to make it. You're gonna live, Henry, and I'm gonna see to it that you answer for what you've done. By God, if it's the last thing I ever do, I'm gonna see to it!"

2

G.W. Braddock rode into Alpine and headed straight toward the two-story red brick courthouse. It was a pretty building with arched windows topped by white trim that stood out against the bricks. Set off to one side and behind the courthouse was a somewhat smaller and less fancy building that resembled it. That would be the jail, Braddock thought.

That was his destination.

He was a tall, lean man who rode easy in the saddle. His skin bore the permanent tan of a man who spent most of his time outdoors. A white scar ran from his forehead up into the sandy brown hair under his pushed-back Stetson. A mustache of the same shade drooped over his wide mouth. He was a young man who looked older than he really was, not an uncommon occurrence in the harsh landscape of West Texas.

As he rode along the main street of Alpine, the only settlement of any size in the vast county that was larger than several Eastern states, he saw the boardwalks were crowded. A low, angry-sounding buzz of conversation came from the throngs. It looked like just about everybody from a hundred miles around was in Alpine today and most of them were mad.

The settlement lay in a broad, relatively flat valley surrounded by gray, hump-backed mountains. Alpine was a ranching community and always had been because the surrounding area was ranching country and not much good for anything else—although there was some cinnabar mining down in the southern part of the county, he recalled, around the little towns of Terlingua, Lajitas, and Study Butte.

The large number of wagons parked along the street and the horses filling the hitch racks confirmed Braddock's hunch that the ranchers from the spreads around here, along with their crews, had come into town. They were there for the same reason Braddock was: to see that justice was done in the case of Henry Pollard.

Of course, their idea of justice likely differed from Braddock's. Most of the people in Alpine probably thought that what Pollard deserved was a short rope and a high tree branch.

Braddock, though, served the law.

He rode around the courthouse and drew rein in front of the jail. A short flight of stairs led up to the entrance and on the small landing in front of the door stood a couple of men holding shotguns. The stars pinned to their shirts shone in the sun.

"Best just stay on your horse, mister," one of them called to Braddock. "You got no business here."

"How do you know that?" Braddock asked. "Maybe I want to talk to one of the prisoners."

"Ain't but one prisoner in this jail right now and he ain't gettin' any visitors."

Braddock frowned and said, "One prisoner? In the whole jail?"

"That's right. Now move along."

Braddock glanced at the windows on the building's first floor and saw that several of them were open. He caught glimpses of movement behind them. He looked up at the roof, which was flat instead of the peaked roof of the courthouse. In a couple of places, rifle barrels poked over the edge. From the looks of things, he guessed he had at least half a dozen guns pointed at him right now.

He raised his voice and said, "Now, don't any of you boys go gettin' trigger happy. I just want to show you something."

Slowly and carefully, he raised his left hand and moved his vest aside so that the badge pinned to his shirt underneath it could be seen. The silver star in a silver circle was instantly recognizable as the emblem of the Texas Rangers.

The deputies might not notice there was a bullet hole smack-dab in the center of the star. Even if they did, that wouldn't make the badge any less real...whether or not Braddock still had the right to carry it.

The two men at the front door looked at each other. One of them muttered, "A Ranger. Didn't the sheriff send for the Rangers?"

"I dunno," the other guard said. "He might've, I reckon."

Braddock let the vest fall back over the badge and smiled slightly.

"Is it all right if I get down off my horse now?"

"Yeah, I reckon," one of the men said. "I mean, sure, Ranger. Come ahead."

Braddock swung down from the saddle and looped the buckskin's reins around the hitch rail. He tugged his hat down a little, hiding most of the scar, and climbed the half-dozen steps. The two deputies moved aside to let him pass.

"Sheriff's office?" he asked.

"Right inside to the left," one of the guards replied.

Braddock nodded his thanks and opened the door. The air in the hallway was hot and still and faintly musty as he stepped inside. He smelled an underlying odor of unwashed flesh and human waste, common to every jail he had ever set foot in.

To his left was a door with a frosted glass panel in its upper half. Gilt letters that read SHERIFF were painted on it. Braddock opened the door and went in.

He found himself in a small outer office with an empty desk in it. A door on the other side of the room led into the sheriff's private office. A bald man with a crisp white mustache stood behind the desk in that room, bent over a little and reaching down as if he were putting something into or taking something out of a drawer. He wore black suit pants, a dark gray vest, and a white shirt buttoned up to the throat without a tie. The vest had a tin star pinned to it. The man straightened, looked at Braddock, and said, "Who're you?"

Braddock moved the vest aside again to let the sheriff see his badge and said, "G.W. Braddock."

"Captain Hughes send you out here?"

"I'm here, aren't I?"

The sheriff frowned and said, "That's mighty fast

action. I only sent that telegram to San Antonio a couple of days ago."

Braddock hadn't known that the Brewster County sheriff had contacted the Rangers asking for help but he wasn't surprised. He said, "I happened to be in Fort Stockton and a wire caught me there. Figured you could use the assistance as soon as possible, so I came right on."

The sheriff nodded, evidently accepting that explanation, and came around the desk to extend a hand.

"John Dearborn," he introduced himself and, as he spoke, Braddock caught a faint whiff of juniper berries. He guessed that the sheriff had been putting a bottle of gin back in the desk when he came in.

Braddock gripped the sheriff's hand and said, "Tell me what we're dealing with here."

Dearborn waved Braddock into a chair in front of the desk. He went back to his own chair, sat down, and took a cheroot from a wooden box on the desk.

"Cigar?" he asked.

Braddock shook his head and said, "I don't smoke."

"Hell, I don't smoke the damn things. I just gnaw on 'em." Dearborn dropped the cigar back in the box, leaned back, and sighed. "You saw the crowd when you rode into town, I suppose."

"Pretty hard to miss," Braddock said.

"Folks have come in from all over the county. Wouldn't surprise me a bit if some of them are even from neighboring counties. This is a pretty sparsely populated part of the state. It takes some doing to put together a real crowd. But everybody within a week's ride wants to be here for the hanging of Henry Pollard."

"That's your prisoner. Your *only* prisoner, according to the men outside."

"I had some other men in custody but the charges didn't really amount to that much. Drunk and disorderly, disturbing the peace, petty theft. By and large, Brewster County's pretty peaceful these days. I asked the judge to commute their sentences to time served, and under the circumstances, he agreed. I wanted to devote all the efforts of my office to keeping Henry Pollard alive."

"I thought you said you were going to hang him."

"*After* he's convicted. We haven't had the trial yet. That's not until day after tomorrow."

"Somebody wants him dead before then?" Braddock asked.

Dearborn snorted and said, "Who *doesn't* want that son of a bitch dead?"

Braddock cocked his right ankle on his left knee, pushed his hat back a little, and said, "Why don't you tell me the whole story?"

3

"IF YOU WANT THE WHOLE THING, IT GOES BACK HALF A year or so," Dearborn said as he laced his fingers together over his belly. "Henry Pollard's brother is Amos Pollard, owns the Triangle P spread. Ever heard of him?"

Braddock shook his head and said, "I've spent most of my time in the brush country, down in South Texas."

"Well, Amos fancies himself the big he-wolf of this part of the country and I suppose that's not far wrong. He was out here when there was nothing but Apaches and scorpions and rattlesnakes and he survived and built his ranch by being meaner than all of them. So, over the years, he's gotten used to riding high, wide, and handsome, and so has his little brother."

"Henry."

"Yep. Henry had a reputation for fighting and boozing and going after any woman who caught his eye, even some who were married. Most folks looked the other way because they didn't want to get on

Amos's bad side. As if he weren't tough enough himself, he's got a pretty salty crew riding for him."

"Men like that put a bad taste in my mouth," Braddock said.

"Mine, too," Dearborn said, "but the thing of it is, generally speaking, Amos Pollard's a law-abiding man. He's always kept his cowboys in line for the most part and whenever they got too rambunctious in town and I had to lock 'em up for a day or two, Amos didn't give me any trouble over it. Even rode in and paid their fines himself. I could live with that."

"But he didn't ride herd on his brother that well," Braddock guessed.

Dearborn sighed and said, "Henry decided he'd taken a fancy to a young woman named June Castle. She lived in a settlement called Santa Angelina, down in the southeastern part of the county. As nice a girl as you'd ever want to meet. Her father owned a store down there. June helped him out and taught school a little, too, whenever there were any kids willing to show up. When Henry Pollard started courting her, she told him she knew his reputation and that he'd have to settle down a whole heap if he wanted anything to do with her. So for a while there, it looked like he was going to do it."

Braddock shook his head and said, "But it didn't last."

"How'd you know that?"

"A man can't change what he is," Braddock said flatly.

"Well, I don't know about that but Henry Pollard didn't change, not really. He got tired of putting on an act, I guess, and one night while they were alone at her pa's house, he tried to force her to...you know.

June wasn't having any part of it and fought back. In the commotion, a mirror broke and June grabbed a piece of that broken glass and cut Henry with it." Dearborn put the tip of his left index finger just below the ear on that side of his face and traced a line down almost to his chin. "Laid his jaw open real good. That would have been enough to discourage most men."

"But not Pollard."

Dearborn sighed again and said, "He took that broken glass away from her and carved her face up pretty bad with it, a lot worse than he was cut. Then he left her there, covered with blood and screaming."

Braddock felt his own jaw clench tight. He said, "Man like that ought to be put down like a mad dog."

"You won't find many who'll disagree with you, Ranger. Anyway, the marshal down there at Santa Angelina, Pete Whitby, rode out to the Triangle P to see about arresting Henry but he wasn't there. Amos claimed he'd sent him away. Said Henry had told him about what happened and it was too raw for even Amos to swallow. He told Henry to get out, that he wasn't gonna protect him anymore. He told Marshal Whitby that Henry lit out, heading east." Dearborn paused, pushed his lips out, and then said, "Most folks believe what really happened is that Amos gave his brother enough money to go hide out somewhere, San Antonio or Austin, maybe, some place big enough that it'd be hard to find him. Myself, I don't really know anything except that Henry Pollard was gone." A bleak look settled over the sheriff's weatherbeaten face. "Then a week ago he came back to Santa Angelina. You probably know what he did there."

"Led a pack of killers into the town. They gunned

down everybody they could draw a bead on and burned almost the whole place to the ground."

Dearborn nodded solemnly. He said, "I figure he put that wild bunch together wherever he's been holed up the past six months. A few of them were killed during the fighting. Border trash, from the looks of them. Bandits and gunmen from both sides of the Rio. A hundred and forty-seven people lived in Santa Angelina. Fifty-one of them died that day and it's a pure miracle there weren't more of them killed than that. By God, Ranger, it was like an act of war!"

Silence hung in the office for a few moments before Braddock asked, "How did you wind up with Pollard behind bars?"

"The deputy marshal down there, a young fella named Tom Nation, wounded and captured him. As soon as Nation saw the scar on his prisoner's jaw, he knew who it was. He shoved a rag in the bullet hole he'd put in Pollard, tied him on a horse, and rode the rest of that day and all night to get him here. There was no place to lock him up in Santa Angelina, you see. The jail had burned down like most of the other buildings. And Marshal Whitby was dead, killed in the raid, so it was up to Nation to deal with Pollard by himself."

"Sounds like a good man," Braddock mused.

"Seems to be. Not much more than a kid but he's got sand."

"It didn't take long for word to get around about what Pollard and his friends had done."

Braddock had heard about it in the village of Esperanza, just south of the Rio Grande, where he had been recuperating from some wounds for the past few months. As soon as he'd heard about how outlaws had destroyed an entire town and wiped out more than a third of its occupants, he had known he would have to cross the border and return to Texas, despite having been warned not to. Somebody had to answer for an outrage like that and making sure justice was served was a job for the Rangers.

Even for a Ranger who was more outlaw than lawman these days.

Braddock had circled around to come at Alpine from the northeast as if he were really riding from Fort Stockton. He had taken the bullet-holed badge from his pocket and pinned it to his shirt. As far as anyone in Alpine was concerned, he really was a Ranger, the job he had been born and bred for. The job that had been taken away from him unjustly because of politics. He didn't see why he had to give it up, not when he could still do what needed to be done.

"Nothing like that has happened out here since the Apaches all drifted down into the mountains in Mexico," Dearborn said. "Even in the old days when they were raiding, I'm not sure there was ever a massacre as bad as what happened at Santa Angelina. So, yeah, the word spread far and wide. Folks think of Henry Pollard like he's some sort of monster." The sheriff shook his head. "I don't reckon you can blame them for that, either."

"You and the judge moved fast to put him on trial."

"Damned right we did. The sooner he's convicted and strung up, the better. But it's got to happen legally. I've been hearing talk for days that a mob's going to take him out of here and lynch him. I'm not going to let that happen, not if I can stop him."

"And that's why I'm here," Braddock said, "to help you protect a mass murderer."

163

Dearborn stiffened, frowned, and said, "It's the law."

"Yes, it is," Braddock agreed. "I'll do everything in my power to see to it that Pollard gets a fair trial and that any sentence is carried out properly."

Dearborn appeared to relax a little. He nodded and said, "I'm glad to hear it, Ranger Braddock. Folks respect the Rangers. Even the way they are now, the Rangers carry a lot of weight."

Braddock's face didn't betray any of the emotions he felt. These days, the Rangers were a mere shadow of the organization they had been until recently. A court decision motivated by political enemies had stripped the Rangers of most of their manpower. Four small companies remained of the legendary Frontier Battalion, each commanded by a captain with six men working under him. Less than thirty men to police the vast Lone Star State. That was a crime in itself and Braddock intended to do everything he could to help make up for it.

He said, "I think maybe there's something you're not telling me, Sheriff."

Dearborn glared and said, "I don't know what you mean."

"What about Amos Pollard? After all those years of looking out for his little brother, you mean to tell me he's just going to stand by and let you hang Henry?"

"If he's convicted in a court of law—"

"You said Amos came out here when there wasn't any law west of San Antonio. A man like that usually believes, deep down, that he's a law unto himself and can do whatever he wants. He protected Henry when he mutilated the Castle girl or at least urged him to run away. That went against the law."

"That was one girl, and she didn't even die." Dearborn grimaced. "I know that sounds callous, but it's the facts. This time fifty-one people died. Men, women, and children. There's no way in hell even Amos Pollard would try to protect his brother from the consequences of that atrocity."

Braddock leaned forward a little and asked, "Are you absolutely sure about that, Sheriff?"

Dearborn stared at him for a long moment and then licked his lips like he wanted to pull that gin bottle out of the desk drawer and take a big swallow from it. Finally, he shook his head and whispered, "No. No, I'm not sure."

4

BRADDOCK PUT HIS RIGHT BOOT BACK ON THE FLOOR
and said, "I'd like to see the prisoner."

"Sure," Dearborn said with a nod. "Sure, we can do
that."

He ushered Braddock out of the office and then led
him along the hall to a staircase.

"The cell block is on the second floor," Dearborn
said. "Makes it harder to jump out a window if a prisoner gets the bars loose somehow. We've got Pollard in
our special cell, though. No windows."

Another shotgun-toting deputy stood at the
bottom of the stairs. He nodded to the sheriff.

"This is Ranger Braddock, Clyde," Dearborn said.

The man nodded and said, "Ranger."

That scene was repeated at the top of the stairs
with the two guards posted there. About twenty feet
along the hall was an iron gate with another guard. At
Dearborn's order, the man produced a ring of keys,
unlocked the gate, and shoved it back. On the other
side was an anteroom with a small desk and a heavy

wooden door. The guard posted there unlocked the door and let the sheriff and Braddock into the cell block.

"Looks like it wouldn't be easy to get out of here," Braddock commented. "Or in."

"That's the idea." Dearborn pointed along a corridor that was lined with empty cells on both sides. "That door down there is Pollard's cell."

The regular cells had doors made of iron bars like Braddock had seen in dozens of jails. The special cell where Henry Pollard was being held had a steel door with a small, barred window set into it.

"Must be pretty hot in there with no windows," Braddock said as he and Dearborn walked along the corridor. Their footsteps echoed hollowly from the jail's thick outer walls.

Dearborn grunted and said, "I don't reckon anybody's going to lose any sleep worrying over how comfortable Pollard is. But there's a ventilation shaft that goes up to the roof. It's too small for a man to get through, and the top is barred, too." They came to a stop in front of the door. The sheriff called through the little window, "Pollard. Somebody to see you."

"My brother?" came the reply from inside.

"No. I still haven't seen hide nor hair of Amos. I don't think he wants anything to do with you anymore."

A face appeared at the bars in the window. The light up here wasn't that good but Braddock could make out the man's angular, lantern-jawed features, topped by a shock of fair hair. He was fairly handsome although the thin scar running along the line of his jaw on the left side of his face made him less so.

"You're wrong, Sheriff," Henry Pollard said as his

lips twisted into a sneer. "There ain't no way Amos is gonna let me rot in here, and he sure as hell won't let you bastards hang me."

"We'll see," Dearborn said.

"Who's this?"

"Ranger G.W. Braddock. He's here to see to it that everything's done proper and legal-like."

Pollard directed his sneering scrutiny at Braddock. He said, "One Ranger?"

"That's generally enough," Braddock said.

Pollard just smirked and laughed.

Braddock moved a little closer to the window and asked quietly, "Doesn't it bother you, knowing you're responsible for the deaths of so many people and destroying a town?"

"They had it comin'," Pollard snapped. "They ran me off, all because some high-toned bitch got what she deserved. Nobody cuts me and gets away with it. But those bastards in Santa Angelina didn't see it like that. They would've put me in jail for doin' what I did. Bunch of worthless little piss-ants. I had to leave my home, but I swore I'd get even with 'em. With that Castle bitch and all the rest of 'em. They'll never forget Henry Pollard."

Braddock let Pollard spew his venom until he ran out of breath. Then Braddock nodded slowly and said to Dearborn, "I've seen what I need to see, Sheriff."

"You mean you're ready to get out of here?"

"More than ready," Braddock said.

Pollard gripped the bars in the window and shouted obscenities after them as they went back along the corridor. Once they were going down the stairs, Dearborn said, "He's crazier than a shithouse rat."

Braddock smiled faintly and said, "I found myself thinking the simplest thing to do would be to put a bullet in his head. Like that mad dog I was talking about earlier. But that wouldn't be according to the law, would it?"

"No, and I reckon we both swore an oath." They paused outside the door to Dearborn's office, and the sheriff asked, "What are you gonna do now?"

"Find a livery stable for my horse and get a hotel room. Even in a situation like this, a mob would have to be liquored up before they'd attack the jail and I figure that means there's no real danger of an attempted lynching until tonight. I'll be here all night, right out front."

"I appreciate that, Braddock. Just the sight of a Ranger ought to make some of those fools think twice if they decide to storm the place. As for the livery, Gardner's is the best place in town. And the Brewster House is the best hotel. They'll take care of you."

Dearborn told him how to find both places, and then Braddock said, "One more thing, Sheriff. June Castle."

"What about her?"

"Was she killed in the raid on Santa Angelina?"

"As a matter of fact, she wasn't. Pollard probably wanted her dead more than anybody else, but she survived." Dearborn paused. "And she's here in Alpine. I reckon she's looking forward to seeing him swing."

———

BRADDOCK TURNED the buckskin over to the friendly proprietor of Gardner's Livery. The man didn't have an empty stall, but he promised to find room for Braddock's horse and take good care of the animal because he was happy to have a Texas Ranger in town.

"I don't mind the crowds, you understand," Ben Gardner said. "Lots of extra business for me. It's just that with this many angry folks in town, the air feels like it does before a summer storm, you know? Like all hell's fixin' to bust loose any time."

Braddock nodded and said, "I know the feeling."

It was much the same at the Brewster House, where the hotel clerk signed Braddock in and said, "We're full up, but I can move some folks around and make room for you, Ranger."

"I don't want to put anybody out. Reckon I could share..."

"Oh, no, that won't be necessary. I'll see to it, don't worry." The clerk nodded toward the Winchester and the set of saddlebags Braddock carried. "In the meantime, you can leave your gear with me. I'll have it taken up to your room when it's ready. I'll make sure it stays safe. Until then, you can wait in the dining room if you'd like, and I'll bring your key to you as soon as I can."

It was getting on toward midday and Braddock was hungry. He nodded and said, "That'll be fine."

The clerk said, "I'm glad we've got a Ranger in town. Sheriff Dearborn's a good man, no doubt about that, but I'm not sure he can keep the lid on this."

Braddock just nodded and turned toward the arched entrance to the dining room.

Most of the tables were full. Several waitresses in gingham dresses and white aprons hurried among them, taking orders and delivering food. Braddock spotted an empty table in the corner, made his way to it, and sat down. He was aware of the eyes following him. He was sure that word had already gotten around town about a Texas Ranger riding in. People were curious about him, even as they were grateful for his presence.

One of the waitresses, a sweet-faced brunette about twenty years old, came over and set a cup of coffee in front of him as he took his hat off and dropped it on the table. Braddock smiled and said, "I didn't order that."

"If you don't want it, I can take it away," she told him.

"I didn't say that. Fact of the matter is, I appreciate it. If you could bring me a steak and some potatoes to go with it, that would be even better."

"Right away, sir."

Braddock sipped the coffee, which was excellent, as the waitress bustled away. He ignored the other people in the room who kept stealing glances at him. Instead, he thought about the situation he had ridden into.

The wire Sheriff Dearborn had sent requesting help from the Rangers might be answered, or it might not be. The tattered remnant of the Frontier Battalion was spread far and wide these days and the simple fact of the matter was that Captain Hughes might not have anybody available to send to Alpine.

But if he did...if another Ranger rode into town in the next couple of days...there was an excellent chance he would know that Braddock wasn't supposed to be wearing that badge. Braddock had broken enough laws in his quest for justice that he'd been warned to stay out of Texas. Yet here he was, unable to stay away when he was needed.

Either way, there wasn't anything Braddock could do about it. Another Ranger would show up or he wouldn't. Fate would follow its own course. That was the way of it.

A sudden awareness that the room had fallen silent broke into Braddock's reverie. He glanced up and saw the reason why.

A woman had come into the dining room and was walking toward the table where he sat. Judging by the silence and the gauzy veil that hung over her face from the flat-crowned straw hat she wore, he figured she was June Castle.

5

BRADDOCK GOT TO HIS FEET AS THE WOMAN CAME TO A
stop beside the table. She said, "Please sit down,
Ranger Braddock." The thin veil obscured her features
but didn't muffle her voice. "You *are* Ranger Braddock,
aren't you?"

Braddock remained standing. He said, "Yes, ma'am."

"I'm Miss Castle."

"Yes, ma'am." Braddock moved a hand toward the
empty chair across from him. "Will you join me?"

"I..." For a moment, he thought she was going to
refuse. There was something tense and expectant
about her, like a bird about to take wing and launch
into startled flight. But then she nodded under the veil
and said, "Yes, thank you."

Braddock stepped around the table and held the
chair for her as she sat down. Most of his upbringing
had been devoted to preparing him for life as a Ranger,
but while his mother was still alive, he'd been taught to
be a gentleman as well.

He looked across the room, caught the eye of the pretty waitress who'd brought the coffee, and angled his head toward June Castle. The waitress nodded her understanding and went to fetch another cup.

Braddock settled back into his chair. He said, "I'm pleased to meet you, Miss Castle."

"You know who I am, then? You've heard my story?"

"I have. I'm sorry."

"For what?" she asked bluntly. "Because I was maimed by a madman? Or because my actions led to the deaths of dozens of people and the ruination of an entire community?"

"None of that was your fault. The blame for all of it lies with that madman you mentioned—Henry Pollard."

June Castle clasped her hands together on the table in front of her. They were slender, long-fingered hands and very pale. She said, "Not everyone sees it that way. There's been talk...Some say that if I'd given in to Henry to start with, like he wanted, none of those awful things would have happened."

"Ma'am, people who would think something like that don't deserve the attention you'd give a mosquito. They're just wrong, that's all there is to it."

"I'm not so sure. Wouldn't it be better to trade one person's pain and humiliation for the destruction of so much else?"

"Those waters are over my head, Miss Castle," Braddock said. "I'm just here to help see to it that Pollard pays the price for what he's done."

"Will hanging him do that? Will hanging him bring back all the people he killed or undo all the destruction? Will it take back this?"

She raised her hands to the veil and lifted it, revealing the ugly red and ragged scars that criss-crossed her face. Braddock was able to catch a glimpse of the beauty that had once been present under those terrible injuries.

She held the veil up only for a second, then as she dropped it Braddock said, "No, ma'am, hanging Pollard won't change any of that. But it's all we've got, isn't it?"

"It's not enough," she whispered.

Braddock sighed and asked, "What would you have me do?"

"If he's tried and convicted, they'll build gallows and drop him through it. It'll be a clean drop, Sheriff Dearborn will make sure of that, he's a good man. Henry Pollard's neck will snap, and his life will be over." June Castle's fingers tightened on each other. "If he's taken out and a rope is thrown over a tree limb to haul him up, he'll strangle. He'll take minutes to die and he'll be in agony. It won't be enough...not nearly enough...but it will be better than the fast, clean death the law will give him."

"So you want me to let a mob lynch him," Braddock said. "That won't change any of what he did, either."

"No...but as you said, it's what we have."

The conversations in the room had started up again, although at a lower level than before. People had gone back to their meals and cast only occasional glances at the Ranger and the young woman sitting at the table in the corner. The waitress came to the table with a cup of coffee, set it in front of June, and asked quietly, "Would you like something to eat, Miss Castle?"

"No, thank you," June said. Her voice was polite but

cold. When the waitress had gone, she asked Brad-dock, "She's pretty, isn't she?"

"I suppose."

"You know she is. She's pretty and I never will be again. And it's all Henry Pollard's fault." Her voice trembled as she spoke.

"Nobody's denying that—" Braddock began, then stopped as he realized someone else was approaching the table. A young man this time, tall and slender with brown hair that tried to fall forward over his forehead. He carried his hat in one hand.

"June," he said as he stopped beside the table, "I thought we were going to eat dinner together."

"Go away, Tom," she told him without looking up. "I'm talking to this Ranger."

The young man looked at Braddock, nodded, and said, "You're Ranger Braddock. I heard you were in town." He put out his hand. "Tom Nation."

Braddock stood up and shook with him.

"You're the deputy from Santa Angelina who captured Pollard."

"Yeah," Tom Nation said. "But I've thought plenty of times since then it might have been better if I'd just gone ahead and shot him." He smiled, but there was no humor in the expression. "I suppose I shouldn't admit such a thing to a Ranger."

"Been plenty of times I've felt the same way," Braddock said with a little smile of his own. "Join us?"

Before Tom could respond, June Castle said, "I've spoken my piece." She stood up and turned away from the table, leaving the cup of coffee untouched.

"June, you don't have to leave," Tom said, but she ignored him. Some of the people in the dining room watched her surreptitiously as she walked out but others stared openly. Tom Nation just sighed.

"Sit down," Braddock said. "No point in letting good coffee go to waste."

"I suppose you're right," Tom said. He put his hat on the table and sat down where June had been.

When Braddock had settled back in his chair, he said, "You deserve congratulations for bringing Pollard in. From what I've heard, you found yourself in the middle of quite a battle."

Tom picked up the cup, sipped from it, and said, "It wasn't a battle. Nobody was able to fight back enough to call it that. It was just murder."

"A few of the raiders were killed and you captured Pollard."

"Luck as much as anything," Tom said with a shrug. "He came mighty close to killing me before I knocked him out. And I couldn't do a thing to help any of the folks in town."

"How many raiders were there?"

"Twenty, I'm guessing. Maybe more. With all the commotion, it was hard to tell. And there wasn't really any time to count them."

"How many were killed?"

"Three."

"And Pollard was captured. Anybody else?"

Tom shook his head and said, "No, that's it. The others got away. Why do you ask, Ranger?"

"That means there are at least sixteen men out there who might not want Henry Pollard to be hanged," Braddock said.

Tom Nation sat up straighter in his chair and said, "You don't think they'd come here to Alpine, do you? You don't think they'd try to break him out of jail?"

"I don't see how anybody can guarantee that. Sheriff Dearborn's worried that a lynch mob might try to take Pollard, but it seems to me that's not the only threat."

Tom ran a hand through his hair and frowned worriedly. He said, "I guess you're right. We've been figuring that Henry used some of his brother's money to hire those gunmen but maybe he didn't pay them all of what he promised them. Maybe they were supposed to get the rest of it after the raid on Santa Angelina. If that's the case, they can't get the rest of their money if he winds up at the end of a hangman's rope."

"And that's still not all of it," Braddock said. "The sheriff's convinced Amos Pollard won't do anything to help his brother but I'm having a hard time believing that. I don't know Pollard but I've run across plenty of old cattlemen like him. If he loves his brother, he won't let the law stand in his way."

"Amos has always been blind to just how bad Henry really is," Tom said. "He's always gotten him out of one scrape after another. This is just the worst one there's ever been."

"So there are three different bunches with good reason to want Henry Pollard out of jail," Braddock said as he leaned back, extended his long legs under the table, and crossed them at the ankles. "A lynch mob, the killers who burned Santa Angelina, and Pollard's own brother and the men who ride for him. I'm assuming the Triangle P crew will do whatever Pollard asks of them?"

"Yeah. They ride for the brand and they've always been about half-wild, some of them not much better than outlaws themselves. Good Lord, Ranger, with all this hanging over your head, what are you gonna do?"

Braddock spotted the waitress coming toward the table with a tray of food in her hand. He smiled and told Tom Nation, "I'm going to eat a good meal and then try to get some rest. It's liable to be a long night."

6

Amos Pollard held a framed photograph in his left hand, a squat glass containing three fingers of whiskey in his right. The picture showed a hawk-faced young man with dark hair and a mustache standing with a toddler in his arms. It might well have been a photograph of a man with his son, but despite the difference in their ages, the two were brothers.

Amos and his brother Henry, more than twenty years ago.

Pollard threw back the whiskey, set the empty glass on the sideboard where he had filled it a moment earlier. He looked at the photograph and said, "You stupid son of a bitch."

He didn't indicate which of the people in the picture he meant. He wasn't sure he knew anymore.

The sound of hoofbeats came through the open window in the room that served as Pollard's office, library, and study. The men he had sent into Alpine were back, he supposed. He had given them strict orders not to get drunk or start any fights. If any of the

180

townspeople gave them trouble, they were to walk away. They hadn't liked that, of course. He didn't hire men who were partial to backing down from trouble. But they were there just to scout out the situation, not to raise a ruckus.

Pollard walked over to the fireplace on the other side of the room and set the framed photograph on the mantel. He was still as straight as the man in the picture. A little thicker through the waist, maybe— but only a little. And the hair and mustache were iron-gray now, instead of black. The hawkish face was still the same, sharp and predatory. He swung away from the fireplace as a knock sounded on the door.

"Come in," Pollard said. The years had given his voice a permanent rasp.

Raymond Harper opened the door. He and Bert Luttrell came into the room holding their hats. Harper, who was the Triangle P's ramrod and who had been with Pollard longer than any of the other hands, said, "We're back, boss."

"I can see that," Pollard snapped. "What did you find out?"

"Trial's set for the day after tomorrow," Harper reported. He was a barrel-chested man with salt-and-pepper hair. "Talk in the saloons is that Henry won't make it that long. Lynch fever's buildin'. I reckon there's a good chance it'll break loose tonight."

Luttrell was one of the older hands, too, although younger than Harper. His curly red hair lay close to his squarish head. He said, "It don't help matters that girl is in town. The one from Santa Angelina."

"June Castle," Pollard said.

"Yeah. She wears a veil when she goes out in public

but folks know what's underneath it. That just gets 'em stirred up more. They keep thinking about..."

"About what my brother did to her," Pollard finished the sentence for him. "You can say it, Bert. We all know what Henry did to that girl."

Harper turned his hat over in his hands and said, "You know they're gonna hang him, Amos." He was the only member of the crew who could call Pollard by his given name. "Whether it's a lynch mob or the sheriff and a hangman after the trial, Henry's gonna swing."

"You think I don't know that?"

Harper cocked his head slightly to the side and said, "Question is, what are you gonna do about it?"

Amos Pollard had been trying to come up with an answer to that question for days now. He swung around and stared out the window at the hills and valleys sprawling away for miles. The ranch house was at the top of a hill and commanded a sweeping view of Pollard's range. All that land. All the power and wealth it represented. And yet none of it had been able to change Henry and make a decent man out of him.

He'd never been called Hank, even as a little boy. That nickname never seemed to fit the solemn-faced lad. Pollard had raised him from an early age after a fever had taken both of their folks. They were first-born and last-born, with four other babes in between who hadn't made it through childhood. But they were survivors and Pollard thought that was responsible for the special bond between them.

But Henry had tested that bond many times over the years. Lord, how he'd tested it!

The first time, Pollard recalled now, had been when Henry was just seven years old. He'd gotten thrown off a pony, and one of the hands had laughed at him. What was the fella's name? Briscoe, that was it. Jack Briscoe. Smarting from the fall, face red with embarrassment, Henry had run into the house, then emerged a few minutes later carrying one of Pollard's revolvers. Who would have thought a kid like that could even lift the gun, much less pull back the hammer and fire it? But that was what he'd done, yelling, "Nobody laughs at me, you bastard!" and letting off a shot at Briscoe. A well-aimed shot, too. The bullet had torn Briscoe's left ear off.

Who could ever expect a thing like that?

Raymond Harper had grabbed Henry and taken the gun away from him before the boy could shoot again. Briscoe had yelled and cussed and hopped around and threatened to beat Henry within an inch of his life, but he shut up quick enough when Pollard showed up to see what the shooting was about. When he heard the story, Pollard had given Briscoe his time and an extra double eagle and sent him packing. Better not to keep him around, he'd decided. Better for Henry to just put the whole incident behind him.

Too bad that hadn't been the last one.

"Amos," Harper said, breaking into Pollard's thoughts, "there's something else you ought to know about."

Pollard turned away from the window and asked, "What's that?"

"There's a Ranger in town."

"A Texas Ranger?"

"Yeah. Fella name of Braddock. He rode in late this mornin'."

Pollard nodded slowly and said, "I'm not surprised. John Dearborn's a good man, but he's in over his head and there's only so much courage you can find in a bottle of gin."

Harper and Luttrell waited a minute more, then Harper asked, "What are we gonna do?"

"What are the men willing to do?"

"Whatever you tell us," Luttrell answered without hesitation. "You know we'd follow you straight into hell, boss."

Pollard considered for a moment more, then asked Harper, "You think there'll be a lynch mob tonight?"

"I believe there's a mighty good chance of it," the ramrod said.

"A lynch mob would hit the front of the jail, more than likely," Pollard mused. "That would be a good time for somebody else to hit the back."

SANTIAGO QUINTERO PACED BACK and forth, chewing on a thin black cigarillo as he looked out across the valley toward Alpine, three miles away. Behind him in the narrow canyon, thirteen men lounged around the camp they had made under the trees along the creek. One of them strolled toward Quintero and said, "Starin' off into the distance ain't gonna get us the money we got comin'."

Quintero turned his head and glared at the man whose name was Robinson. He said, "I know that. But is it worth dying over?"

Robinson shrugged and said, "Money's the *only* thing worth dyin' over."

Most of the men gathered here felt the same way, Quintero knew. They were hired killers, the lot of them, accustomed to risking their lives for wages. In fact, three members of the group had died in Santa Angelina, and another had succumbed to his wounds here in the canyon where they had camped while they tried to figure out what to do. Another man had ridden away, declaring that he wasn't going to throw his life away for a hundred and fifty bucks.

Henry Pollard had promised each of them three hundred dollars, plus whatever they could loot from the bank, for a few minutes' work. Ride in, shoot up the town—and the townspeople—and then burn the place. An easy job.

And, in truth, it had been. Some of the citizens of Santa Angelina had put up a fight but most had been too busy trying to save their own lives. Once half the buildings were ablaze, the men had ridden away, ready to collect the second half of their pay.

That was when they realized Henry Pollard was no longer among them. They had turned and gazed back toward the thick column of black smoke rising into the sky and realized he was somewhere in that inferno and the rest of their money was going up in smoke with him.

Of course, as it turned out, that wasn't the case. Quintero, as the nominal leader of the group, had sent one of the men into what was left of Santa Angelina the next day. Meeker, so young and fresh-faced that no one would take him for a cold-blooded killer, had pretended to be a drifting cowpoke who'd come up on the tragic scene. He had hung around all day, helping clean up debris, and learned that the local deputy had captured Pollard and taken him north to Alpine, the county seat, to be locked up in the jail there.

More scouting, this time in Alpine, had confirmed that Pollard was indeed being held there. The trial had been set and there was absolutely no doubt that within an hour of its conclusion, Pollard would be swinging at the end of a rope. The smartest thing to do would be to ride away and forget about the rest of the payoff they were supposed to collect.

The money they had taken from the bank had turned out to be disappointingly skimpy, though, especially divided up among all of them, and the same thought had occurred to Quintero and the other men: Pollard's brother had given him money to hide out, money that Pollard had used to hire men to help him carry out his twisted revenge.

How much more would the elder Pollard pay for his brother's rescue from the hangman?

It was too intriguing an idea to simply cast aside.

Robinson said, "Why don't we ride into town and see where things stand?"

Quintero grunted.

"I think the people will notice so many men riding in, especially men who look like we do."

Robinson looked like a killer, all right, a buck-toothed man with lank blond hair sticking out like straw from underneath a flat-crowned black hat. He said, "I ain't talkin' about the whole bunch. I figured you and me could go in and get the lay of the land. The rest of the fellas can wait for our signal. We'll let 'em know when it's time to hit the jail and grab Pollard. Then we sell him back to his brother and get ourselves a real payoff for a change."

Quintero thought it over. He hated to admit that Robinson was right about anything but what the gringo said made sense. He turned and looked at the other men. Four of them were *Mejicanos* like him, the rest white. Bandits, rustlers, murderers, rapists. As sorry a bunch as any man could cast his lot with.

Yet cast his lot with them, Quintero had. He was no better than any of them and worse than some. The only difference was that his brain was not quite as dulled by debauchery as theirs and, from time to time, the realization of just how evil he really was crept into his thoughts. He didn't like that and usually drowned it quickly with tequila.

"All right," he told Robinson. "Tell the others. We have watched wagons and riders coming into Alpine for days now. The town will be crowded. No one will pay attention to two more men."

"Now you're talkin'," Robinson said, exposing his prominent teeth in a grin. "All we need's a little bit of luck and, in a day or two, we'll be rich men, amigo."

Quintero doubted that. True riches always eluded men such as them. Real wealth settled in the hands of men like Henry Pollard's brother. The rest of them got what was left. But that was what they deserved, Quintero supposed. Were they not the dregs of the world?

As long as they had enough for liquor and whores and ammunition, that was all they really needed.

7

"WHAT'S WRONG, DEAR?" GEORGE'S MOTHER ASKED AS George's pa pushed his plate away and stood up. "You don't like the food?"

"The food's fine. I just don't have much of an appetite." George's pa looked at him and went on, "Boy, you come outside with me."

George felt a chill go all the way through him like a blue norther. His ma turned pale and asked her husband, "What do you want with George?"

"We got business, him and me."

"Any business you have, you can handle in here. It's dark outside."

George's pa ignored that and told George, "I'll be waitin' for you. Don't make me come back in and get you."

He stalked out of the cabin.

George sat there in the rough-hewn chair like he was stuck to it. The last thing he wanted to do was get up and follow his father outside. Yet he knew that he had to. If he didn't, it would just make things worse.

The chair legs scraped on the floor as he pushed it back.

"No!" his mother cried. She clutched his arm. "Don't go out there. I'll talk to him—"

"It won't do no good," George said. He stood up and gently pulled his arm out of his mother's grip. The sickness that was wasting her away had cost her most of her strength, so she couldn't hold him even though she was grown, and he was ten years old.

"George..."

He forced his legs to move and walked out into the dogtrot between the two halves of the cabin. He shut the door behind him, hoping his ma wouldn't follow him. He knew what this was about and he didn't want her to see it.

His pa was standing out in the moonlight, smoking. When George said, "I'm here," he dropped the quirly at his feet and ground it out with the toe of his right boot.

Then he turned, a dark, massive shape, and said, "I stopped at Kincaid's store when I was comin' back through town this afternoon. Kincaid told me you and your ma were there this morning."

"That's right," George said. He had driven the wagon in and he'd been proud of himself for doing it. They had needed supplies and they didn't know when Pa would be back. They never knew how long he'd be gone when he was off Rangering. As it turned out, they could have waited because he'd shown up late that afternoon.

"Kincaid told me something else. I reckon you know what I'm talking about. You want to tell me?"

Again, George knew it wouldn't do any good to be stubborn. He said, "I guess Mr. Kincaid told you I took a piece of candy without payin' for it."

"That's what he told me," Pa said softly.

Unexpected anger flared up inside George and took away some of the fear. He said, "Did he tell you I chopped wood and hauled water and loaded supplies and ever' other

189

thing he could think of to pay him back? Did he tell you he made me work five hours to settle up for a penny piece of candy?"

"What it's worth don't matter. You stole. That's against the law."

Foolishly, George said, "You gonna arrest me? Write my name down in your Book o' Knaves?"

He didn't see the big open hand coming in time. It slammed against the side of his head and knocked him sprawling, half in and half out of the dogtrot. Pain hammered inside his skull as he lay there. He tried not to cry but he couldn't keep from whimpering.

"I don't like to do this," his pa said, "but you done wrong and you got to be punished."

Fiery agony slashed across George's legs. He tried to squirm away but his pa came after him, arm rising and falling as the quirt in his hand shredded George's trousers and the skin underneath. George screamed. He couldn't escape.

Light splashed across him as his ma threw the cabin door open and rushed out. She shouted her husband's name and grabbed his arm as yet another blow fell. If she wasn't strong enough to hold George, she sure wasn't strong enough to stop Pa.

But he stopped anyway and backed off, his chest rising and falling heavily, his face set in stony lines.

"How could you?" she screeched at him. "How could you do that to your own son?"

"He stole," Pa said. "Everybody's somebody's son or pa or brother. It don't matter. You break the law, you got to pay the price."

BRADDOCK WOKE UP THRASHING, as he often did. The bedding was wet with sweat and wadded up like a dog had been digging around in it. Braddock pushed himself up into a sitting position and waited there for his rapidly slugging heartbeat to settle down.

When the hammering of blood inside his skull had subsided somewhat, he drew in a deep breath and rubbed a hand over his face, which was beaded with oily perspiration. The room was hot, with the curtains drawn tightly over the single window to shut out the light but that wasn't what had made Braddock sweat so much. Rather it was the memories lurking inside him, the ones he kept tamped down deep enough that they could escape only in dreams.

He said, "Shit," swung his legs out of bed and stood up.

A table with a basin and pitcher of water sat against the wall. Braddock poured water into the basin, scooped some up in his hands, and splashed it over his face. The coolness made him feel a little better. He lifted the pitcher and drank straight from it. That helped, too, although his stomach felt a little sick for a moment when the water hit it.

When his legs were steadier, he crossed to the window and shoved the curtains back. The light outside had started to dim because it was late afternoon, almost evening. It was still bright enough to make Braddock wince. He muttered something that didn't make sense even to him and turned away from the window to pull his clothes on.

Ten minutes later, he walked into the hotel dining room. The young woman who had waited on him earlier was still working. Once again, she brought coffee to him without being asked.

"You're an angel in disguise," Braddock told her as he picked up the cup.

That brought a laugh from her. She said, "Hardly. You should ask my pa. To hear him tell it, I'm nearer to the Devil."

"Sometimes it's hard for those closest to us to see the truth."

"I suppose so. You want a bowl of chili, Ranger?"

"The hotter the better," Braddock said.

"The way our cook makes it, it'll scorch your insides."

"That's just what I need."

If the chili could burn away all those old memories, that would be even better but Braddock knew not to expect that much.

Feeling almost human again after he'd eaten, Braddock went up to his room and got his Winchester, then left the hotel and headed toward the jail. The sun had set behind the jagged mountains to the west and dusk was starting to gather over Alpine.

The town was still busy. Light and noise spilled from the buildings, especially the saloons. Anticipation hung in the air. It was almost a festive feeling, like a celebration was about to begin.

A celebration of death, Braddock thought, because that was what it would bring if most of the people in town tonight had their way.

But somewhere out there were others who wanted to forestall that death and the chances were good that he would have to deal with both sides before the night was over.

Maybe he could improve those odds, he thought as he came to the Rainbow Saloon which appeared to be one of the largest such establishments in town. It was certainly one of the noisiest although the level of that racket dropped off sharply as Braddock pushed through the batwings and walked toward the bar carrying the rifle.

He felt the weight of every eye in the place as he came to a stop in front of the hardwood. He tucked the Winchester under his left arm and nodded pleasantly enough to the man behind the bar.

"Your beer," he said. "Is it cold?"

"Coldest you'll find around here," the sallow-faced bartender replied.

"All right, then," Braddock said. "I'll have one."

"Sure, Ranger." The man filled a mug with frothy liquid and set it in front of Braddock. "No charge."

"No, I pay my way," Braddock said. He slid a silver dollar across the bar. "Good enough?"

"Sure." The bartender made the coin disappear. "You've got more comin' if you want it."

Braddock picked up the mug and took a long swallow. The beer was cool, almost cold, and tasted good. He set it down and said, "Looks like you're doing a pretty brisk business."

"Lots of people in town these days," the bartender said.

"I expect they've come in for Henry Pollard's trial."

"Yeah," the bartender said but Braddock heard the hollow insincerity in the man's voice. "That's why they're here."

Braddock took another swallow of the beer and said, "Better be. *I'm* here to see to it that things go off like they're supposed to. Legally and proper-like. Nothing else is going to happen while I'm in Alpine."

"Sure, Ranger," the bartender said. "Don't know

why you'd expect otherwise. Folks around here are law-abiding. Most of them, anyway."

"I just want to make sure everybody understands." Braddock drank again, then left the half-full mug on the hardwood. "Anybody who tries to cause trouble will be dealt with by the full force of the law."

His voice was loud enough to carry in the hush that had fallen over the saloon.

The bartender didn't look happy that Braddock had come into his place to issue the veiled warning. His face was tight and angry as he said, "You've spoken your piece, Ranger. Anything else I can do for you?"

"Nope." Braddock turned and headed toward the entrance.

He hadn't gotten there when a man stepped out in front of him, blocking his path. The man was as tall as Braddock but burly in comparison to the Ranger's lean, panther-like build. He wore range clothes, including a black-and-white cowhide vest, and his face was flushed with both drink and resentment.

"You're in my way, friend," Braddock said with deceptive mildness.

"Now I've got somethin' to say," the man declared. "You come in here and act all high an' mighty 'cause you're a Ranger, but that badge on your shirt don't mean a damn thing to me. If you were a real lawman, you'd want Henry Pollard to swing at the end of a rope and the sooner the better!"

Mutters of agreement came from all over the crowded saloon.

"There's no doubt in my mind that's where he's going to end up," Braddock said. "*After* he's been tried and convicted."

"That's a damn waste of time!" the cowboy said.

"Anyway, the longer he sits there in jail, the more likely it is his blasted brother will try to bust him out! Amos Pollard's been runnin' rough-shod over this part of the country for twenty years. What makes you think he's gonna follow the law this time?"

This time there were a few cheers and whistles in response.

"Because I'm going to see to it," Braddock said when the hubbub had quieted down. "Now get out of my way, mister, so I can do my job, or you'll find yourself behind bars, too."

Something flickered in the cowboy's eyes, a wish that he hadn't pushed things quite this far, maybe.

But he had, and he was too proud to back down, so he exclaimed, "You go to hell!" and swung a fist at Braddock's head.

8

THE COWBOY WAS JUST DRUNK ENOUGH FOR THE BOOZE to slow him down. Braddock had no trouble leaning out of the way of the roundhouse punch. As the cowboy lost his balance and stumbled a step closer, Braddock brought up the Winchester and laid the stock along his jaw, not with enough force to break bone but hard enough to put the hombre on the floor.

Braddock swung around and dropped the Winchester's barrel so that it pointed in the general direction of several angry-looking men sprang to their feet at the tables where they'd been sitting.

"Everybody just hold your horses," Braddock said, his voice ringing out clearly. "By all rights, I ought to arrest this man for trying to attack a peace officer." He nodded toward the cowboy who lay stunned on the sawdust-littered floor. "I'm not going to. I understand why folks around here are upset. *But the law will be upheld.* Henry Pollard will go on trial as the law requires. And if anybody tries to interfere with that..."

Braddock backed to the batwings. "It won't go as easy with them."

He stepped out into the gathering night, knowing that word of this encounter would spread swiftly through the town. Maybe it would make enough men think twice to blunt the rising tide of lynch fever. He wasn't going to count on it, though.

His long-legged strides carried him quickly toward the courthouse and jail. He was about a block away when muzzle flame gouted from the darkness across the street and he felt as much as heard the whipcrack of a bullet past his ear.

The shot took him by surprise. He knew plenty of people in Alpine probably resented his presence in town but he hadn't thought any of them would go so far as to try to bushwhack him. As another shot blasted, he dived off the boardwalk into the thick shadows behind a parked wagon. The second bullet thudded into the vehicle's sideboards.

Braddock had seen where the shots were coming from. He stood up and fired three fast shots over the wagon toward the alley where the ambusher lurked. It was too dark in there to see anything but he figured if he sprayed some lead around, the would-be killer might abandon the attempt and flee.

Another bullet smacked into the wagon as he ducked but this one came from a different direction. Braddock felt splinters sting his cheek as the slug struck close to his head. He twisted around and dropped back, landing on his butt. A handgun roared from the corner of the nearest building and sent another bullet shrieking just over his head.

"Hey!" a man yelled. Another gun went off. Braddock jerked his head to the right and saw a third man running across the street toward the second bush-whacker. The revolver in his hand belched flame.

Since someone had taken a hand on his side, Braddock rolled onto his belly and socketed the Winchester against his shoulder. From that position, he fired underneath the wagon bed this time and sent three more rounds into the alley across the street.

No one returned that fire. Either he had downed the first bushwhacker or the man had taken off for the tall and uncut.

Boots pounded on the boardwalk. Braddock swung the rifle in that direction. A familiar voice called, "Hold your fire, Ranger! It's me, Tom Nation!"

Along the street, men were cursing and shouting questions. They began to venture out cautiously to see what was going on. Braddock hoped any innocent folks on the street had gotten safely out of the line of fire.

He got to his feet but kept the wagon between him and the alley just in case.

"Over here, Deputy," he told Nation.

Still holding a Colt, Tom came up to him and asked, "Are you hit?"

"No. They came close but not close enough. How about you?"

"They never even tried for me," Tom said. "They sure did want to kill you, though, from the looks of it."

"How did you happen to show up just at the right time like you did?" Braddock asked. He had no reason to be suspicious of Tom Nation, but caution was ingrained in him.

"I saw you come out of the Rainbow and head toward the jail. I was across the street. I was going down there, too. Figured I'd volunteer to help stand guard tonight. Then I saw those bushwhackers open up on you and knew I had to pitch in and help."

"I'm obliged to you for it, too," Braddock said. "They had me in a crossfire of sorts. Don't know if I could have gotten out of it."

"Did you get a look at either of them?"

"No. How about you?"

Tom shook his head and said, "No, all I saw was a shape running off."

A new voice called, "What the hell's going on down there?"

"That's Sheriff Dearborn," Tom said. He raised his voice. "It's Tom Nation, Sheriff, and Ranger Braddock."

Dearborn stalked up to them with a shotgun in his hands. He wore his suit coat now, as well as a bowler hat. He demanded, "Blast it, why are you two shootin' up the town?"

"A couple of men tried to ambush me, Sheriff," Braddock explained. "The deputy helped me run them off."

"You know who they were?"

"No...but it's a safe bet there are plenty of folks in town who don't want me here."

Dearborn grunted and said, "I wouldn't think most of 'em would have the guts to take a shot at a Ranger, though."

Braddock felt the same way. He said, "I don't suppose it matters. What's important is that they missed. We'd better all get down to the jail while we can."

"Yeah," Dearborn said. "A storm's fixin' to break if I ever felt one."

SANTIAGO QUINTERO and the gunman called Robinson rendezvoused where they had left their horses tied in a small clump of trees a quarter of a mile outside Alpine. Quintero was mad because the bullet burn on the side of his face stung like blazes. He realized, though, how close he had come to dying tonight, so he was grateful that the man who had come to the Ranger's aid wasn't a slightly better shot.

Robinson appeared to be in worse shape. He was limping and muttering curses under his breath as he entered the shadows under the trees.

"You're hit?" Quintero asked him.

"What the hell do you think?" Robinson snapped. "One of Braddock's shots grazed my leg. I got my bandanna tied around it to stop the bleedin' but it still hurts like the dickens."

Both of them had been in the Rainbow Saloon when Braddock came in to put on his little show. In their low-voiced conversation, they had decided that no matter what they wound up doing, it would be easier if the Ranger were out of the way.

So as soon as Braddock left, they had slipped out a side door and split up, hurrying to get in position to ambush him. If the light had been a little better...if Braddock hadn't been so lucky...if that other son of a bitch hadn't come along and taken cards in the game...the Ranger would be dead now.

But there was no point in thinking about what might have been, Quintero knew. A smart man dealt with the world the way it really was, not how he wished it could be.

Robinson leaned against a tree trunk to ease his painful leg and asked, "You still think there'll be a lynch mob tonight after Braddock warned folks like that?"

"I do," Quintero said. "Some hombres will back out because they do not want to face a Ranger, but there will be enough who are drunk and stubborn and proud. That man Braddock knocked down, he'll want revenge. He'll be one of the ringleaders. My gut says it is so."

"Yeah, I think you're right. What do we do now?"

Quintero thought it over for a moment, then asked, "Can you ride?"

"Hell, yes, I can ride," Robinson answered without hesitation. "I've been shot worse than this and rode all day."

"Then go back to the canyon. Get your leg patched up. Then bring all the men back here and watch for my signal to attack the jail."

"What's that gonna be?"

Quintero thought again, then said, "I saw a church with a tall bell tower. I'll take a lantern up there and light it, then swing it back and forth three times. When you see that, you'll know to bring in the men. I'll be waiting for you at the back of the jail. The Ranger and the sheriff and the rest of the lawmen will be at the front, trying to keep out the mob. They won't know we're there until it's too late."

Despite the pain of his injury, Robinson grinned, his prominent teeth visible in the shadows.

"And then Pollard's brother makes us all rich men," he said, "or we'll string up the little bastard ourselves!"

9

Sitting stiff and straight in the saddle, Amos Pollard rode in the forefront of the group of men headed toward Alpine. Raymond Harper was a little behind and to his right; Bert Luttrell occupied the same position to the left.

Behind them came eighteen more riders, the bulk of the crew from the Triangle P. Pollard had left his cook, wrangler, and blacksmith behind, along with three of the other hands. They were older, somewhat stove up, but all good men. If any trouble came up, they would be able to deal with it.

Most of the hands had been with Pollard long enough that he could sense their mood. He knew that misgivings ran deep in some of them. Over the years, they had been involved in plenty of minor scrapes with the law but they didn't like the idea of possibly having to shoot it out with the sheriff, his deputies—and a Texas Ranger.

Others, though, were ready, even eager, for trouble.

For the chance to cut loose their wolf and show that Triangle P wasn't to be messed with.

But whether they were apprehensive or raring to go, more than likely they all wished they were setting out on a more worthwhile mission than the rescue of such a sorry specimen as Henry Pollard. Amos knew that and the knowledge gnawed at his guts like a coffin worm.

The lights of Alpine were visible in the distance. Harper edged his horse forward until he was even with Pollard and said, "What's the plan when we get there, Amos?"

Pollard had always been a decisive man, not the sort to ask advice from anyone. But with uncertainty strong in him tonight, he said, "Tell me, Ray...do you think there's any chance in hell John Dearborn would let Henry go if I asked him to?"

Harper blew out a breath and said, "The kid's responsible for a bunch of people dyin' and a whole settlement bein' burned to the ground. It ain't like the scrapes he got into before. It ain't even like the time he...did what he did to the Castle girl. How can Dearborn let him go?"

"Dearborn's a coward."

"He's been out here damn near as long as you have, Amos. He's fought his share of Apaches and rustlers and Mexican *bandidos*, just like you."

"That was twenty years ago," Pollard said harshly. "He's gotten old and soft. He realizes he doesn't have all that many years left and he doesn't want to lose them. That's why he crawls into a gin bottle every chance he gets. It helps him forget that, every time he lays his head on the pillow at night, he's one day closer to the grave."

Harper didn't say anything for a long moment, then, "You're probably right about that but I still say he won't back down. Besides, he's got that Ranger there to keep his backbone a mite stiffer. He's got his regular deputies and some extra men he took on and that kid lawman from Santa Angelina who captured Henry is still around, too. If you ride up and tell Dearborn to turn Henry loose, he'll refuse and then he'll put up a fight when you go to take the boy out."

"Then we'll do like I said. We'll wait until the mob comes up to the front of the jail, and while Dearborn's dealing with them, we'll go in the back. There'll probably be just a couple of men on the rear door. They won't stop us."

"And men on the stairs and up in the cell block, too," Harper warned.

"They'll get out of our way."

"And if they don't?"

"Then God help them."

"Amos...by the time this is over...the law's liable to be after *you*, too. No offense, but are you willin' to give up everything you got, just to...well..."

"To save my brother? My no-good brother who's got the blood of dozens of innocent people on his hands?"

"Like it or not, those are the facts," Harper said.

"I'm getting Henry out of there and that's the end of it," Pollard said. "If you don't like it, Ray, I won't hold it against you if you turn back."

Harper snorted disgustedly and said, "Nobody's turnin' back. We're Triangle P and we're in this to the hilt."

THE JAIL WAS MOSTLY dark when Braddock got there with Dearborn and Tom Nation. The first thing he said was, "You need to get some light on the grounds so you can see what you're shooting at, Sheriff, if it comes to that."

"If we're shooting, it'll be at citizens," Dearborn said.

"If they try to take a prisoner out of jail, they're lawbreakers."

"Yeah, that's what I keep tellin' myself. I keep tryin' to believe it, too." Dearborn sighed. "But you're right. I'll get some lanterns out here."

"Around back, too."

The sheriff frowned and said, "Seems to me like a lynch mob would come to the front door."

"Unless the mob was just a distraction."

Dearborn looked at Braddock for a moment and then nodded. He said, "I should've thought of that myself. Guess I'm gettin' too old for this job."

Braddock didn't say anything about that. Instead, he asked, "Do you still have riflemen on the roof?"

"Yeah, a couple."

"Put two more men up there. Have each one cover a side."

"All right." If Dearborn objected to a Texas Ranger coming in and taking over the defense of the jail, he didn't show it. He went on, "I've got six men armed with pistols and shotguns inside the jail tonight."

"Regular deputies?"

"Some of them are. Others are specials I hired until after the trial."

"All of them are from here in town?"

"That's right," Dearborn said.

Braddock didn't say anything but his brain was

working quickly. He didn't like the way things were adding up. If a mob stormed the jail, the guards would be asked to shoot at men who were friends and neighbors, maybe even relatives. All to protect a man who didn't deserve anything except a guilty verdict and a rope. Braddock had seen for himself just how loco Henry Pollard was. There was no one in Alpine tonight who deserved to die protecting the likes of Pollard.

And yet the law demanded it. Things had to be done in a certain way in order to be right. Braddock had always believed that.

At least until he'd pinned on a badge he no longer had a right to wear...

He forced that thought out of his mind. His own actions didn't matter tonight. What was important was getting through this with the smallest loss of life possible.

Dearborn was looking intently at him. The sheriff said, "You're thinking that my men won't fight, aren't you?"

Dearborn might be past his prime but he wasn't stupid. Braddock said, "If you were a special deputy, or even a regular one, would you want to gun down your best friend to protect Pollard?"

"No, but they swore an oath—"

"A lot of men swear oaths. They doesn't always mean much when your finger's on the trigger and you're looking over a gun barrel."

"Well, then, what the hell do we do?" Dearborn demanded in exasperation.

It seemed to Braddock there was only one answer and it depended on someone else.

He turned his head to look at Tom Nation and

wondered just how much he could ask the young deputy to do.

QUINTERO OPENED the door of the First Methodist Church and went inside. His footsteps echoed slightly in the sanctuary. A couple of lights mounted on the wall gave off dim light. The church appeared to be empty.

That was good. Quintero might be a cold-blooded killer but he didn't like the idea of slaying a man of God. He wouldn't even want to knock out such a man and tie him up.

The gunman carried a lantern he had stolen off someone's back porch. He had swung it back and forth to check for the slosh of fuel and knew it had enough oil in it for his purpose. He looked around, found a door to a small room with a narrow ladder in it that led up to the bell tower.

He was glad the church had a tower like this, instead of a steeple. That wouldn't have done him any good. He hung the lantern's bail over the barrel of the Winchester he also carried, then started up the ladder, a bit awkwardly because of his burden.

A trapdoor at the top swung up and let him climb out onto a narrow platform around the big bell itself. Quintero lowered the trapdoor and set the lantern on it. Then he had a look around.

The view was good from up here. He could see practically the entire town. The front of the jail was visible from where he was and it sprang into sharp relief when he took a telescope from the pocket of his charro jacket, extended it, and squinted through its lens. The telescope was army issue, taken off a dead cavalry officer a couple of years earlier, and worked well.

Lanterns hung from the posts that held up the roof over the small landing at the top of the jail's entrance stairs. More lanterns had been set out here and there so that the area in front of the jail was, if not bright as day, at least bright enough for the men inside the building to draw a bead on the members of any lynch mob.

The front door was closed and the landing was empty. The jail's defenders had already forted up inside.

Quintero raised the spyglass and focused on the roof. A smart sheriff would have riflemen posted up there and, sure enough, even though the glow from the lanterns on the ground didn't reach the roof, Quintero spotted starlight winking off rifle barrels. He couldn't tell how many men were on the roof but there were several, for sure.

From here, with his own Winchester, he could pick them off before they knew how or why they were dying.

Quintero lowered the telescope and turned his attention to the brightly lit saloons. Even from up here, he could hear the racket coming from them, a low rumble that sounded angry and menacing. Now and then louder shouts could be heard, followed by cheers.

The rotgut was flowing like a river tonight, Quintero thought with a tight smile. The saloons were full of men guzzling down that liquid courage. When they had braced themselves with enough of it, when they had worked themselves into a frenzy of vengeance directed at Henry Pollard, they would pour out into the night and head for the jail.

And it appeared that was going to happen sooner rather than later, Quintero saw. A knot of men appeared at the entrance of one of the saloons and erupted into the street like a boil being lanced. Matches flared to life and were held to kerosene-soaked torches. Flames shot up, casting a hellish glare along the street. More and more men came out to join the first ones. In a matter of minutes, a mob of at least fifty men had formed and it continued to grow as they started toward the jail.

Quintero picked up the lantern he had brought into the bell tower, fished a match of his own from his pocket, and lit it with a snap of his fingernail. He held the flame to the lantern's wick, and when it was burning well, he lowered the glass chimney, took hold of the bail, and held out the lantern so Robinson and the other men would be able to see it from their hiding place outside of town. He swung the light back and forth three times, then blew out the flame, set the lantern down, and picked up the rifle from where he had leaned it against the low wall around the outside of the tower.

Now all he had to do was wait for the killing to start.

Braddock and Dearborn were sitting in the sheriff's office with the lamps unlit when one of the deputies who been posted outside appeared in the open doorway and said, "They're comin', Sheriff."

Braddock rose from the chair where he'd been leaned back in an apparently casual pose with his right ankle propped on his left knee. His hat was pushed to the back of his head. He pulled it down now so the brim was square with his face. He picked up the shotgun he had set on the sheriff's desk. Dearborn picked up his Greener as well.

The sheriff sighed and said, "Reckon there's no stoppin' it now."

"We won't know that until we try," Braddock said.

They followed the deputy to the jail's front door. Another man stood there, tense in the light that came through the windows from outside. He asked, "What do you want us to do, Sheriff?"

"Be ready at the windows," Dearborn said. "Shoot if

you have to—but nobody in here fires the first shot. You understand that?"

Both guards nodded. Their hands shifted on the shotguns they held, changing from one grip to another and then back again.

Braddock leaned over slightly to peer out a window at the mob approaching the jail along the side of the darkened courthouse. A number of them carried torches, which wasn't very smart of them. The added light just made them easier targets.

Something about a mob, though, demanded torches. It was in the nature of the beast.

Based on the clothes they wore, some of the men were townies while others were cowboys from the spreads in the area. All of them wore angry, determined expressions. Some didn't appear to be too steady on their feet. Those would be the ones who'd imbibed a little too much liquid courage.

Braddock spotted the cowhide vest of the man he'd laid out earlier in the Rainbow Saloon. The man was in the front rank of the mob. Braddock pointed him out to Dearborn, asking the sheriff, "Who's that fella in the black and white vest?"

"That's Vince Franklin," Dearborn said. "Has a little spread south of town."

"Is he married?"

"Yeah," Dearborn replied. Braddock heard the worry in his tone. "He and his wife have a couple of kids."

The corner of Braddock's mouth tugged in a grimace. He didn't care for the answer he'd gotten, but there was nothing he could do to change it.

The mob was only about twenty yards away now.

Dearborn sighed and said, "Reckon I'd better go out there and talk to them."

"I'll do that," Braddock said.

"No, you won't," Dearborn said with a trace of unexpected steel in his voice. "I'm still the sheriff of Brewster County."

Braddock looked at the man in the dim light of the jail's foyer and then nodded.

"All right, Sheriff. But I'll be right behind you. Right beside you if you need me."

"And I'm obliged to you for that."

Dearborn grasped the doorknob and swung the door open. He blocked the entrance, standing squarely on the jamb.

"You men stop right where you are!"

His words held a commanding tone as they rang out over the open area in front of the jail. The members of the mob slowed, took another step or two, and then stopped as if it were against their will but they were unable to go on.

"You know why we're here, Sheriff!" one of the men holding a torch called. "Step aside and nobody has to get hurt."

"You know I can't do that, Joe," Dearborn told the man. He stood stiff and straight with the shotgun held in both hands at an angle across his chest. "You fellas don't have any business here tonight. Just turn around, go on back to your homes, and we'll forget this ever happened."

"To hell with that!" The angry bellow came from Vince Franklin. "You got a killer in there who's got to pay for what he done, Sheriff!"

"Henry Pollard will pay," Dearborn insisted, "once a

jury has convicted him and a judge has passed sentence. Not before."

"Everybody here knows that's what's gonna happen," another man in the forefront of the mob said. "What's the difference?"

"The difference is, it hasn't happened yet. If you string up Pollard tonight, it won't be justice. It'll be murder!"

That accusation brought a wave of angry shouts from the mob. Franklin said, "Whether it's tonight or day after tomorrow, he's still gonna hang!"

Dearborn nodded curtly and said, "That's right, Vince. So what difference does it make? Why does it have to be tonight?"

"Because we're tired of waitin'!" Franklin shouted. "And because Amos Pollard's liable to come into town any time with that crew of renegades who ride for him and turn his brother loose!"

Again the crowd yelled its agreement.

Dearborn shook his head stubbornly and said, "If Amos Pollard shows up, I'll tell him the same thing I'm tellin' you boys. Henry is gonna stand trial and anything that's done will be carried out proper and legal-like."

Franklin leaned over and spat derisively.

"Nobody out here believes that," he declared. "You're too old, Sheriff. You're scared you're not gonna make it to that rockin' chair you got waitin' for you."

Dearborn stiffened even more. He lowered the shotgun so that it pointed in the general direction of the mob. That brought angry mutters but some of the men began to look nervous and eased back a little, especially those in the front ranks of the crowd.

"Vince, you'd better get out of here right now," the

sheriff warned, "or else your wife's liable to become a widow and those two young'uns of yours won't have their pa anymore."

For a second, Braddock saw indecision, maybe even fear, on Franklin's flushed face. But then the outrage came back, stronger than ever, and he started toward the jail as he opened his mouth to say something. Dearborn swung the shotgun's barrels toward him.

There was no telling what might have happened if shots hadn't blasted out from the back of the jail at that moment.

QUINTERO WAS KNEELING on the platform in the bell tower with the barrel of his Winchester resting on the low wall. He pressed his beard-stubbled cheek against the smooth wood of the stock and peered over the barrel at the roof of the jail. The rifle's sights were lined up on the guard covering the rear of the building. The unlucky bastard didn't know it but he had only moments left to live.

When the first shots sounded, telling him that the mob had attacked the jail, Quintero stroked the trigger. The Winchester cracked and Quintero saw the guard pitch forward as the slug punched into his back. The man toppled off the roof and disappeared.

Quintero worked the rifle's lever, shifted his aim, and fired again. Another of the rooftop guards went down. Quintero smiled as he jacked another round into the chamber.

It always felt good for a man to use his skills productively.

BRADDOCK WHEELED AROUND and ran down the long hallway leading to the back of the building. He'd been expecting something like this all along but it appeared that the attackers had jumped the gun a little. If they had waited a moment longer, the jail's defenders would have had their hands full with the mob.

As it was, Franklin and the other men were now milling around in confusion, unsure of what was going on and not knowing if they should storm the jail or scatter and hunt some cover.

Braddock didn't know what he would find back there: Amos Pollard and the men from the Triangle P or the killers who had accompanied Henry Pollard in the bloody raid on Santa Angelina.

It didn't matter. Whoever was trying to get in, Braddock intended to stop them.

He was still twenty feet from the rear door when it exploded inward—literally. The blast blew Braddock off his feet. *Dynamite!* he thought. He hadn't expected that. As he scrambled up, still holding the shotgun, he saw men charge in through the ragged opening where the door had been. Muzzle flame flickered in the hallway as they fired blindly.

Braddock yelled, "Now!" and touched off the Greener's right-hand barrel. Smoke and flame gushed from the weapon as deadly buckshot shredded the invaders.

At the same time, more shots came from the rear staircase to the right and the office to the left where Braddock had posted deputies. The men who had been standing guard outside had been ordered to retreat at the first sign of an attack and join the others. That had drawn in the raiders. The dynamite had been an unexpected—and unnecessary—tactic. Braddock *wanted* the men to get inside.

The first men through the door were caught in a crossfire between the staircase and the office and knocked down by buckshot and pistol and rifle rounds. Other men, not knowing what was happening but determined to breach the jail, replaced them and ran into a similar storm of lead. Braddock dropped to a knee, aimed the shotgun, and fired the second barrel into the chaos of curses and muzzle flashes. He tossed the empty scattergun aside and palmed out his Colt. It roared and bucked in his hand as he triggered three shots.

The few attackers who were still on their feet broke and ran.

Braddock surged up and dashed to the opening along with several of the deputies. He emptied his revolver after them as did the men with him. Some of the fleeing attackers went down. Braddock wasn't sure how many of them vanished into the darkness. No more than one or two, he thought.

"Stay here," he snapped at the deputies. "Guard this hole."

Then he turned and ran toward the front of the building. There was still the startled mob to deal with.

HALF A MILE OUTSIDE ALPINE, AMOS POLLARD ABRUPTLY
reined his horse to a stop as he heard the rattle of
gunshots, followed closely by the dull thud of an
explosion.

The other men had halted, too, and Bert Luttrell
exclaimed, "What the hell!"

Raymond Harper sucked on a front tooth and then
said, "Sounds a mite like a war."

"A mob's trying to get to Henry," Pollard said. He
jammed his boot heels into his horse's flanks and sent
the mount leaping forward. Over his shoulder, he
called, "Come on!"

The others galloped after him. As he rode, fear
welled up his throat and threatened to choke him.

Were they too late? By the time they made it into
town, would Henry's lifeless body already be dangling
from a rope thrown over a tree branch?

If that turned out to be the case, Pollard would
have his vengeance. He would make the town sorry for

this night. That would be one more turn in the bloody cycle of death but he swore it anyway.

WHEN BRADDOCK REACHED the jail's front door, he saw right away that the gunfire and the explosion had caused the mob to splinter and come apart. At least half of the men had scattered and the ones who remained, including Vince Franklin in his cowhide vest, had pulled back and taken cover behind the trees beside the courthouse. Braddock heard Franklin's loud, abrasive voice as he urged his companions to regroup and attack the jail.

Dearborn had retreated just inside and to the left of the open door. He still held his shotgun and had the barrels trained on the open area in front of the jail. He turned his head to glance at Braddock and asked, "Are you all right?"

"I'm fine," the Ranger replied as he moved up next to the door on the other side, staying out of the line of fire if any of the men outside started shooting. "As far as I know none of your deputies were hit, either, at least not bad."

"What the hell was that explosion?"

"Whoever tried to get in back there used dynamite on the door." A grim smile flashed across Braddock's lean face. "I didn't figure on that. But it didn't help 'em. They charged right into the crossfire I had waiting for them."

"Any of them get away?"

"One or two, maybe."

"Was it Amos Pollard and his men?"

"I don't know," Braddock said, his voice bleak. "All I saw was corpses."

Dearborn nodded and said, "I was hopin' the ruckus would make everybody in that mob decide to light a shuck. I think they might have if it hadn't been for Franklin. He rallied some of 'em."

"He's the ringleader, all right," Braddock agreed. "That's why if anybody can put a stop to this, it's him."

Dearborn looked at him with narrowed eyes and asked, "What are you thinkin' about doin'?"

"I think it's time to let Franklin know what the situation really is." Braddock leaned closer to the door and called, "Franklin! Vince Franklin! This is Ranger Braddock! I want to talk to you!"

The muttering from the men who had sought cover outside stopped. After a moment of silence, Franklin replied, "Unless you're gonna tell me you're ready to turn Pollard over to us, Ranger, there ain't no use in talkin'!"

"I think there is," Braddock insisted. "I'm coming out there. I want you to meet me and we'll talk, man to man."

"The way we talked earlier in the saloon, when you hit me with that rifle?"

"You swung at me first," Braddock said. "And I could have arrested you but I didn't."

Again there was silence. Braddock hoped that Franklin was actually considering what he'd said, rather than plotting something else. Finally, after several tense moments, Franklin called, "All right, Ranger, I'll talk to you! But this better not be a damned trick!"

"It's not," Braddock replied. "I give you my word on that."

As the Ranger stepped into the open doorway with his hands empty and raised slightly, Dearborn said, "You'd better be careful, Braddock. Tempers are still runnin' pretty high out there, I'd say."

"I intend to be," Braddock said.

He moved out onto the landing and then went down the steps to the ground. As he did, Franklin stepped into the open, too, from behind the tree where he had taken cover earlier when the shooting started.

Braddock glanced around as he walked forward. He spotted a dozen more members of the mob crouched behind cover here and there and figured there were probably that many he couldn't see. He was out in the open, a good target if somebody decided to start the ball again. He hoped that once he talked to Franklin, though, and told him what the real situation was, the shooting would be over.

The two men stopped about ten feet apart, still within the circle of light cast by the lanterns in the trees around the jail and the courthouse. Franklin glared at Braddock and snapped, "Say whatever it is you've got to say, Ranger, so we can get on with this."

"There's nothing to get on with," Braddock said.

"That's where you're wrong. Henry Pollard's gonna swing before this night is over."

Braddock shook his head slowly and said, "I don't think so. He's not even here."

———

ABOUT A HUNDRED YARDS from the edge of town, Amos Pollard slowed his racing mount as Harper came alongside him again and said urgently, "Amos, hold on!

You need to listen. The shootin's stopped. Whatever was goin' on, it's over."

Pollard brought his horse to a stop and stared toward the courthouse and jail. He could see the glow of lights around them.

"It can't be," he said in a choked voice. "We can't be too late."

"Maybe we ain't." Harper leaned forward in the saddle. "Let me go on the scout. You and the rest of the fellas stay here. I'll get closer and see what I can find out."

Pollard looked over at his foreman and old friend and said, "You might be risking your life."

"Shoot, that's what we set out to do, ain't it?" Harper asked with a wry grin. "Anyway, riskin' one man's life is better than riskin' everybody's."

"I'll come with you—" Pollard began.

"No, it's better you stay here. Somebody might see you and recognize you and then that'd be liable to start a ruckus by itself. Folks'd be bound to think you were there to bust Henry out of jail."

Pollard knew that Harper was right. As high as the sentiment was running against him and Henry, if any of the townspeople laid eyes on him, they might start shooting just on general principles.

"All right," he said with a sigh. "We'll wait here. But you be careful, Ray."

"Didn't I scout for the Army, back before I went to work chasin' cows for you? I know how to skulk around, boss, don't worry about that."

Harper clucked to his horse and rode slowly toward town. Shadows soon swallowed him.

"I don't like this, boss," Luttrell said from behind Pollard.

"I know," Pollard said. "I don't like any of it. Something just doesn't feel right..."

"NOT EVEN HERE?" Vince Franklin repeated as he stared at Braddock in disbelief. "What kind of loco yarn are you tryin' to spin, Ranger?"

"It's not a yarn," Braddock said. "It's the truth. I moved Henry Pollard out of here earlier and had him taken to a safe place."

Franklin stared at him for a second and then shouted, "That's a damned lie!"

Anger stiffened Braddock's spine. He said, "Normally, I wouldn't take that, Franklin. This is the second time tonight I'm letting you get by with something. There won't be a third."

"I don't believe it." Franklin shook his head stubbornly. "You're still hidin' him in there. Why you'd go to so much trouble and risk your life for a man who's done the things Pollard did, I just don't understand."

"Maybe I don't, either," Braddock said quietly, "but that's the way it is. If you don't believe me, will you believe the evidence of your own eyes?"

Franklin's voice was thick with suspicion as he asked, "What do you mean?"

Braddock jerked his head toward the jail and said, "Come on inside and see for yourself. Look anywhere in there you want to. Check everywhere in the building. You'll see that Pollard's not there."

Braddock's voice was loud enough that the other members of the mob who were still around the jail could hear him, too. That was what he wanted. Once the men realized their cause was hopeless, maybe they would give up and go home.

Franklin was still suspicious. He said, "You're just tryin' to get me in there so you can take me prisoner and use me as a hostage."

"No, he's not," Sheriff Dearborn said as he marched out of the jail and came toward Braddock and Franklin. "You go with the Ranger, Vince. I'll stay out here so your friends will know that we're playin' straight with you. If you don't come back, they'll have *me* to use as a hostage."

One of the other men called to Franklin, "Go ahead, Vince. See if the Ranger is telling the truth."

Franklin looked like he didn't care for the idea at all but he nodded and said, "All right, Braddock. You show me what you've got to show me."

"Look for yourself," Braddock invited. He turned and started toward the jail. Reluctantly, Franklin followed him.

They went up the stairs and into the foyer. Franklin cast a wary glance at the armed deputies.

Braddock said, "All the cells are upstairs, but you're welcome to look around down here if you want to."

"Let me see the cells," Franklin said.

Earlier, Braddock had made sure all the cells were unlocked, as well as the iron gate and the cell block door. He led Franklin up the stairs and into the cell block. The rancher looked into every cell as they passed but it was obvious Henry Pollard wasn't in any of them.

"That's where the sheriff had him locked up," Braddock said as he pointed to the special cell at the end of the corridor. The door was ajar and, as they reached it,

Braddock took hold of the door and pulled it open all the way, revealing the empty cell.

Franklin had a lost, confused look on his face now. He stepped into the doorway of the special cell and looked around as if to make sure Henry Pollard wasn't hidden in a corner. Franklin turned to Braddock and asked, "What the hell did you do with him?"

"Like I said, he's in a safe place," Braddock replied. "But don't worry. The law's still going to deal with him."

"THAT'S FAR ENOUGH, POLLARD," TOM NATION SAID. "We'll rest the horses for a spell."

"You're crazy, trying to ride through these mountains at night," Henry Pollard said. "One of us is gonna fall in a ravine and break our neck for sure."

"If it happens to you, it'll just be a little sooner than it would be otherwise," Tom said.

As soon as the words were out of his mouth, he sort of regretted them. He had known Ranger Braddock for less than twelve hours but already the Ranger had impressed on him the need for doing things according to the law. Tom had already felt that, but Braddock had reinforced it.

That was why he and Henry Pollard were miles north of Alpine now, riding through the Davis Mountains toward the town of Fort Davis. The settlement was the county seat of Jeff Davis County and had a nice sturdy jail. That was where Pollard would be locked up until the judge could come up from Alpine and preside over his trial, which would take place on schedule in another couple of days, only in a different location than originally intended. It was called a change of venue, Braddock had said, and was perfectly legal.

As soon as it was dark, Braddock had had four horses brought to the back door of the jail. A couple of them were extra mounts that Tom and Pollard would switch to later because Braddock expected them to ride all night and reach Fort Davis by morning.

"As soon as things have settled down here, I'll come after you if I can and try to catch up," Braddock had said. "But I know you'll get Pollard through even if I don't, Tom."

"How can you know that?" Tom had asked. "You barely know me."

The Ranger hadn't hesitated before saying, "I trust my judgment and it tells me you're up to the job. You're the one who brought in Pollard in the first place, after all."

Tom considered that mostly luck but he hoped Braddock was right. Anyway, there wasn't much choice. Getting Pollard out of Alpine was the safest course of action, not only for the prisoner but also for the people who might try to bust him out of jail and lynch him. If that happened, innocent men would be killed. Well, maybe not entirely innocent, if they'd joined a lynch mob, Tom mused, but he still didn't want them to die.

This way, they wouldn't have any reason to.

As the two of them sat there letting the horses blow, Pollard said, "You know you'll never get me to Fort Davis, don't you, Deputy? My brother will come after me. He'll find out where you're taking me and he'll set me free."

"I wouldn't count on that," Tom said. "Braddock was pretty careful. I don't think anybody saw us leave the jail and, as we were riding out of town, we were just a couple of drifting hands, nothing special for anybody to pay attention to."

Pollard's hands had been tied to the saddle horn and his ankles were roped together under the horse's belly. A gag had been shoved into his mouth and tied in place so he couldn't yell and draw attention to himself as they were leaving town.

He didn't have any reason to want to do that since the lawmen were trying to save him from a necktie party but, with somebody as loco as Henry Pollard, you couldn't ever predict what he might do. It didn't have to make sense to anybody else as long as his fevered brain told him it was the right thing to do.

"I don't care," Pollard insisted. "You'll see. You'll never get me there. You'll die out here. Die screaming."

"Shut up or I'll gag you again," Tom muttered.

Pollard laughed. He said, "You like bein' a hero, don't you, Deputy? You're the big man who brought in the loco killer. I'll bet all the girls think you're something to swoon over now." Pollard paused, then went on, "But you don't really care about them, do you? You're only interested in one *special* girl."

"I warned you, you better shut up," Tom said.

Pollard cackled and said, "Hell, I remember now! I remember how at the socials in Santa Angelina, you were always hangin' around June Castle and making eyes at her. You were sweet on that teasin' little bitch, weren't you, Deputy Tom?"

"That's enough, damn you!"

"Bet you wouldn't be sweet on her now if you saw her face," Pollard went on. "Bet you wouldn't be able to look at her without pukin' your guts out! But I guess you could always put a tow sack over her head while you were lovin' on her—"

Tom was too furious to think straight. He turned his mount and crowded it against Pollard's, and the back of his hand cracked across the other man's face as he swung his arm in a vicious blow. The impact jerked Pollard's head to the side. His body swayed in the same direction but he couldn't fall off the horse because of the way he was tied into the saddle.

"Shut up!" Tom yelled. "Shut your filthy mouth, you cold-blooded bastard!"

Pollard righted himself and grinned in the starlight. He said, "I'm just tellin' you what you already know. But you don't know this, Deputy...That time she cut me, before she got her hands on that piece of broken glass...I had her." Pollard's mouth twisted in a sneer. "That's right. I got what I wanted from her—and she loved it. You should'a heard her screamin' my name, boy! It was only afterward she realized what she'd done and got mad at me. That's why she came after me. She was trying to cut my throat so I could never tell anybody what she done, the prissy little—"

With a bellow of rage, Tom went after Pollard again. This time he used his fist, slamming several punches into the prisoner's face as he yelled, "Shut up, shut up, shut up!"

Then the horses, spooked by the commotion, shied apart, and Tom couldn't reach Pollard anymore. He grabbed the saddle horn to steady himself and sat there with the pulse pounding in his head like an artillery bombardment.

A few yards away, Pollard sat on his horse laughing thickly with a black smear of blood around his mouth.

He said, "You can whale on me all you want, Deputy, but it ain't gonna change the facts. That pretty little gal you were sweet on is ruined in more ways than one!"

"She'll never be ruined to me," Tom panted.

"Well, it don't really matter. Before this night is over, my brother is gonna kill you."

———

VINCE FRANKLIN still looked stunned and angry as he and Braddock emerged from the jail. Franklin had insisted on checking every nook and cranny on both floors of the jail before he was forced to admit that Henry Pollard wasn't there.

At the sight of Franklin, several men from the lynch mob came out from the trees where they had taken cover. One of them asked, "How about it, Vince? Is Pollard really gone?"

"He's gone, all right," Franklin admitted. "They snuck him out of town, just like the Ranger said." He turned his head to glare at Braddock. "It ain't right! This is where he should've been strung up!"

"He'll still get what's coming to him," Braddock said. "In the end, isn't that what matters?"

And even then, it wouldn't change anything or bring any of the dead back, he thought.

One of the townsmen said, "Hell, if Pollard's not here, we might as well go home."

"That's the first smart thing you've said all night, Bob," Dearborn told the man.

There was considerable grumbling but the remaining members of the former lynch mob started to disperse. Franklin looked around wildly, probably sensing that his temporary hold on power was gone, and exclaimed, "Hold it! Wait a minute, fellas, we can't let them get away with this."

"There's nothin' we can do, Vince," one of the men told him. "It's over."

"That's right," Braddock said. "It's all over."

"No!" Franklin said. "No, there's gotta be a way to find out where they've taken Pollard..."

None of the other men paid attention to him. They didn't look back as they drifted off into the night.

Dearborn said, "You should go on home to your wife and kids, too, Vince. And be damned glad tonight didn't turn out any worse than it did."

Franklin looked around. He was alone now—and one man couldn't make up a lynch mob.

He wasn't quite ready to give up, though. He pointed a finger at the sheriff and blustered, "This county's had enough of your high-handed behavior, Dearborn! Come the next election, you're gonna be out of a job!"

Dearborn's laughter had a bitter edge to it. He said, "What the hell makes you think I'm gonna want it anymore?"

Franklin didn't have an answer for that. He glared some more but then finally trudged away.

Dearborn sighed and said, "We'd better go around back and see who tried to get in that way. I'm afraid of what we're gonna find."

"That it was Amos Pollard and his men?" Braddock asked.

"Amos is an important man in this part of the country. If he's dead, it'll cause quite a stink."

However, it took only a minute to determine that all of the dead men littering the rear hallway of the jail and the grounds behind it were strangers to the sheriff. He studied their faces in the light cast by the lantern he held up and said, "Don't reckon I ever saw any of them before. They're not Triangle P hands, that's for sure."

"More than likely the hired killers who attacked Santa Angelina with Pollard," Braddock said. "I figured they might try to bust him out. Either he still owed them money or they planned to sell him back to his brother—or both."

"You said some of them got away?" Dearborn asked.

"One or two."

"Then we don't have to worry about them anymore."

Braddock hoped that was the case but he couldn't be absolutely certain of it.

"What are you gonna do now?" the sheriff went on.

"Try to catch up to Deputy Nation and his prisoner," Braddock said. "I'd like to make sure that they get where they're going safely."

"I meant what I said about not running for sheriff again, Ranger. I've had it with this job. I'm too old for it."

As if to prove that he no longer cared, Dearborn slipped a flask from a pocket inside his jacket, unscrewed the cap, and took a long swallow from it.

"That's your business, Sheriff, not mine."

"I appreciate everything you've done here, Braddock," Dearborn said as he lowered the flask. "If it wasn't for you, there's a good chance a heap of innocent men would have died tonight."

"The night's not over," Braddock said.

13

By the time Santiago Quintero made it to the jail from the Methodist church, after climbing down from the bell tower, everything had gone to hell. The fighting was over and the plan he and Robinson had hatched had fallen apart.

Quintero stayed in the shadows of an alley behind the jail, looked at the bodies sprawled between him and the building and just inside the blasted-out entrance, and wondered if all of his compadres were dead. That would be a shame...

But he was alive and that was all that really mattered, after all.

He was about to fade back into the alley, deeper into the shadows, then go back to his horse and leave Alpine behind him. There would be another job somewhere else for a man who was good with a gun and didn't care who he used it on.

Before he could go, a voice hissed at him. Quintero's gun was halfway out of its holster before the man he couldn't see said his name.

Quintero relaxed a little and whispered, "Robinson? Is that you?"

"Over...here."

Quintero followed the voice over to the nearest building, a shed of some sort. His keen eyes picked out a deeper patch of darkness that turned into a shape huddled against the wall as he approached. Just in case, he slipped his iron from leather.

"Robinson?"

"I'm...hit," came the rasping reply.

"How bad?"

A humorless chuckle. Robinson said, "Bad enough."

Quintero dropped to one knee. He leaned closer and smelled something he recognized: the coppery scent of freshly spilled blood.

"The lawmen shot you to pieces, didn't they, amigo?"

"Yeah...The sons of bitches...were ready for us. We got inside...without any trouble...but they caught us in...a crossfire. Somebody...was smart."

"That damned Ranger, I'll bet."

"More than...likely."

"Maybe I'll kill him for you someday."

"I'd be...obliged." Robinson groped in the darkness for Quintero's arm, found it, clutched it with desperate strength. "Don't let me die," he begged. "Don't let..."

He sagged back and his hand slipped off Quintero's arm. Quintero heard the final breath rattle in Robinson's throat. He stood up, hoping that Robinson hadn't gotten blood on his sleeve.

Again, he started to leave, figuring it was time for him to drift but something stopped him. Some instinct that made thoughts stir in his brain. The effort to free Henry Pollard had been a spectacular failure but some good might come of it yet. Now that the jail's defenders had defeated Quintero's compadres and, from the looks of it, routed that lynch mob as well, they were bound to relax. They would think that the trouble was over for the night.

He was safe here in the dark, for the time being Quintero told himself, and it wouldn't cost him anything to wait and see what was going to happen next.

Who knew...only *El Señor Dios*...there might still be something that he could turn to his advantage.

THE WAIT for Harper to return was probably the longest wait of his life, Amos Pollard thought as he sat there on his horse, dreading the news that his old friend might bring him.

The sound of hoofbeats approaching made his back become rigid. His heart clogged his throat. He was anxious to find out what Harper had to report but, at the same time, he wished he could postpone the knowledge longer.

He had suffered through all manner of hardships in his life, he reminded himself. Whatever happened, he would get through it even if he had to call down death and destruction on his enemies to make things right.

"It's me," Harper called a moment later when he was close. "You boys keep your fingers off the trigger."

"Come on in," Pollard told the foreman. Harper loomed up out of the darkness, a tall shape on horseback. "What did you find out?"

"Henry's alive," Harper said, delivering the most important bit of news first. Pollard felt a surge of relief start to go through him but then Harper went on, "He ain't in Alpine anymore, though."

"Not in Alpine? What the hell are you talking about, Ray? They've got him locked up in the jail."

Harper shook his head and said, "Not anymore. That Ranger slipped him outta town. Sent him off somewhere with that kid deputy from Santa Angelina."

"Then what was all that shooting we heard? And the explosion?"

"I slipped up alongside the courthouse and stayed in the shadows," Harper said, not answering the question directly. "They couldn't see me but, from where I was, I could make out most of what Braddock and Sheriff Dearborn were sayin'. As far as I could tell, the fellas who tried to get in the jail and bust Henry out were the ones who went with him to Santa Angelina. You know, the gun-wolves he hired to..."

"I know what he did," Pollard snapped as Harper's voice trailed off. "Nobody has to remind me." He sat there frowning in thought for a long moment, then asked, "Where did they take Henry?"

"Don't know. Braddock didn't say. But he did tell the sheriff he was gonna try to catch up to the deputy. As soon as I heard that, I headed back here right away. Seems to me that if we trail the Ranger, he'll lead us right to Henry."

This time Pollard's brain worked swiftly as he considered what Harper said. He concluded almost immediately that the foreman was right. Braddock was now the key to finding Henry and saving him from his fate.

His well-deserved fate, most would say...but Pollard wasn't going to dwell on that.

He nodded abruptly and said, "All right. We'll follow him. You, me, and Bert."

One of the riders said, "What about the rest of us, boss?"

"Go on back to the Triangle P," Pollard ordered. "There's no telling how long this chase will last and I won't leave the ranch with only a few men there."

"You're liable to need our help," another cowboy protested. "The spread ought to be fine. The Apaches are all down in Mexico, the border's been quiet—"

"And there's no way to know how long it will stay that way," Pollard cut in. "I've devoted decades of my life to that ranch. I won't leave it unprotected. Ray and Bert and I can handle a couple of lawmen, especially since one of them is an inexperienced boy."

"Yeah, but the other one's a Texas Ranger," Luttrell said uneasily. "You're the boss, though—boss."

"Damn right I am," Pollard snapped. He lifted his reins. "And there's no time to waste. Ray, Bert, come with me. The rest of you light a shuck for home."

He nudged his horse into a lope toward the lights of town and didn't look back to see if his men were following his orders.

They'd damned well better be, he thought.

———

BRADDOCK WENT to the hotel to gather the rest of his gear before setting out after Tom Nation and Henry Pollard. Sending the young deputy by himself to take the prisoner to Fort Davis was worrisome but Braddock had thought it would be easier for them to get out of Alpine without being noticed that way. As it turned out, that seemed to have been the right decision. There hadn't been any commotion around their departure.

There was also the chance that Henry would try to escape but Braddock trusted Tom to be as careful as possible. The biggest risk would be when it came time to switch to the extra horses.

Braddock came down the stairs with his saddlebags draped over his shoulder and the Winchester in his left hand. He spotted June Castle, unmistakable in the hat and veil, sitting in a chair on the other side of the lobby. She stood up and moved to intercept him as he started toward the hotel's entrance.

"Ranger Braddock," she said.

"Ma'am." This wasn't a conversation Braddock particularly wanted to have but it seemed there was no avoiding it.

"The talk is all over town that you let Henry Pollard go."

"If that's what people are saying, they've got it wrong," Braddock replied.

"He's not locked up in the jail anymore, is he?"

"No, but he's still in custody. He's still going to be put on trial to answer for what he's done."

"Do you really think Tom Nation can handle a man like Henry?" A bitter laugh came from under the veil. "Henry Pollard is a monster, Ranger Braddock. He's more animal than human. And Tom is only a boy."

"Deputy Nation is a grown man," Braddock said. "He'll do fine."

"If you honestly believe that, you're a fool," June lashed at him. "You might as well have unlocked his cell and let him waltz out, free and clear. And now he's out there somewhere. He's going to come back and...and there's no telling what he'll do..."

Her hands came up, went under the veil, and covered her ruined face as she began to weep.

Braddock grimaced. Like most men, he would have rather faced a war party of Comanche or a gang of owlhoots than a crying woman. He said, "I had to stay in Alpine and deal with the trouble here but that's over now. I'm going after them. I'll see to it that Pollard gets what's coming to him. You have my word on that, Miss Castle."

"It's not good enough," she said between sobs. "Nothing will ever be good enough..."

"I'm sorry."

There was nothing else Braddock could offer to comfort her. He stepped around her, left the hotel, and headed for the livery stable to pick up the buckskin.

14

NOBODY IN ALPINE KNEW SANTIAGO QUINTERO, SO HE was able to walk openly on the streets, trailing the Texas Ranger called Braddock from the jail to the Brewster House. He lingered outside, rolling a cigarette, and smoking it while he propped a shoulder against one of the posts holding up the awning over the boardwalk. He had heard Braddock tell the sheriff he was going after the deputy he had sent out of town with Henry Pollard, so it ought to be a simple matter to trail the Ranger to wherever he was going.

From time to time, he turned and looked through the hotel's front window. After a while, he spotted Braddock coming down the stairs. A woman sitting in the lobby got up to talk to him as he started toward the door.

Quintero frowned slightly as he watched the two of them. The woman wore a veil and the gunman couldn't help but wonder if she was the one who had given Henry Pollard that scar on his jaw. The one he had cut up with a piece of broken glass.

Pollard had told Quintero and the others all about it when he hired them to wipe out Santa Angelina. Quintero hadn't really cared why Pollard had a grudge against the town. The money Pollard had promised them was all Quintero was interested in and he suspected the other men felt the same way.

Pollard didn't seem to realize that and Quintero doubted it would have stopped his boasting, even if he had. Pollard seemed to regard getting his revenge as some sort of unholy quest.

He was loco as a rabid skunk, no doubt about that. But his brother was rich.

Quintero turned and sauntered along the street as Braddock emerged from the hotel. The gunman kept checking over his shoulder until he was sure that Braddock was going to the livery stable. Then he ducked into an alley and kept an eye on the place.

Things would have been a lot simpler if he and the late, unlamented Robinson had been able to kill Braddock when they ambushed him earlier. Quintero didn't think Sheriff Dearborn would have been able to stop them from getting into the jail and freeing Henry Pollard. Most of the men would still be alive and they would be on their way to Amos Pollard's ranch with their prize by now.

But it hadn't worked out that way and Quintero would have to make the best of the situation. He was good at that. He'd always been able to land on his feet, like a cat.

Braddock emerged from the livery stable riding a buckskin horse. He trotted past the alley where Quintero was hidden and headed north out of the settlement.

Quintero raced back to where he'd left his horse

and swung up into the saddle. He was a few hundred yards behind Braddock as they rode toward the tail end of the Davis Mountains.

———

AMOS POLLARD HAD no way of knowing which direction the Ranger would go when he left Alpine, so all he could do was make an educated guess. Pollard was certain that Braddock would have told the deputy to take Henry to one of the surrounding county seats so he could be held in the jail there but which one? Sanderson to the east? Marfa to the west? Fort Stockton to the northeast?

No, Pollard decided, the closest place Deputy Nation would find a good jail to lock up Henry was in Fort Davis, about 25 miles to the northwest through the Davis Mountains.

When he explained his thinking to Harper and Luttrell, the two men agreed with him. Harper nodded and said, "I reckon that's the most likely place they'd go, all right, boss. You want us to circle around town and pick up Braddock's trail when he comes along?"

"Maybe we ought to grab him and use him to trade for Henry," Luttrell suggested.

Pollard considered that idea, then shook his head.

"It's tempting but, until we know exactly where Henry and that deputy are, I don't want to risk them slipping away from us. We could try to make Braddock tell us but I'm not sure we'd have much luck forcing a Ranger to talk."

Harper nodded and said, "They can be pretty stubborn, from what I hear."

"He'll lead us right to Henry, though, I'm sure of it,"

Pollard went on. He hoped he wasn't grasping at straws. That uncertainty bothered him. He had never been a tentative man, not about much of anything. Being absolutely convinced that he was right was one of the things that had allowed him to not only survive the rigors of the West Texas frontier but also to thrive.

The three men rode wide around Alpine and reined their horses to a stop on a bluff about a mile north of town that overlooked the trail leading to Fort Davis. As they sat there, leaning forward in their saddles to ease muscles that weren't young anymore, Luttrell asked, "You don't think he's already gone by and gotten ahead of us, do you?"

"As fast as I got back to you fellas from town, that ain't likely," Harper said.

"We'll wait a spell," Pollard decided. "If Braddock doesn't come along, we can always go ahead and set out for Fort Davis. That would be a gamble—we could be wrong about where they're taking Henry—but we may have to run that risk."

Again, the wait was nerve-wracking, but at least, this time, it didn't last as long. The three men had been waiting on the bluff for about a quarter of an hour when the sound of a horse's hooves drifted through the night to them. Pollard craned his neck to look down at the trail below them which was visible in the light from the moon and stars.

"There he is," Pollard breathed as a man on horseback came in sight. "Can you see him well enough to be sure that's Braddock, Ray?"

"Yeah, it's him, all right," the foreman replied. "Can't really see his face that well but that fella's the right size and shape."

They let the Ranger ride on past and then disappear around a bend in the trail. Unable to contain his impatience, Pollard started to urge his mount forward.

Harper thrust out an arm to stop him and said in a low, urgent voice, "Wait a minute, Amos. There's somebody else comin.'"

Pollard hauled back on the reins and watched as another rider trotted along the Fort Davis trail. This one appeared to be a Mexican, judging by the steeple-crowned sombrero and charro jacket he wore.

"Who in blazes is that?" Luttrell asked in a whisper.

"There's no tellin,'" Harper said. "Could be somebody who don't have anything to do with Henry—or Braddock."

"What are the odds of that?" Pollard snapped. "He's following Braddock, just like we planned to."

Harper shrugged and said, "You could be right. What do you want to do, Amos?"

"Whoever he is, he's trailing Braddock." Pollard jerked his head in a nod as he came to a decision. "We'll follow him."

He heeled his horse into motion again. The animal slipped a little but managed to negotiate its way down the rocky slope. Harper and Luttrell were close behind the cattleman.

When they reached the trail, they turned in the same direction Braddock and the unknown rider had gone.

"Not too close," Pollard ordered. "We don't want them to realize that they're being followed. That could ruin everything."

He realized that whatever happened in the next few hours, it would in all likelihood decide his brother's fate once and for all.

243

T OM N ATION HAD BEEN TRYING to figure out exactly how he was going to handle transferring Pollard from one horse to another. It would have been a lot simpler if he'd had another man here to hold a gun on the prisoner while Tom was cutting him loose and getting him mounted up again.

But he was going to have to accomplish that task by himself, and there was no easy way to go about it except one, as far as he could see.

He told himself to handle it in the dispassionate way a lawman should and not take any pleasure in what was going to happen. Deep down, though, he knew that was going to be difficult.

The stars had wheeled through the sky, the moon had risen and climbed to its height, and Tom knew the hour was well after midnight. He figured he and Pollard were at least halfway to Fort Davis, having followed a well-defined trail that twisted alongside creeks, crossed valleys, and climbed through passes in the rugged terrain.

As they came to a straight stretch of trail alongside a fast-flowing creek bordered by towering cottonwoods, Tom reined in and told Pollard, "All right, that's far enough for now."

Pollard sneered at him and asked, "What are you gonna do, string me up from one of those cottonwood branches?" He mumbled a little because his lips were swollen from the punches Tom had landed on them earlier.

"You know better than that. When you hang—and you *will* hang—it'll be from a gallows with a real hangman doing the honors."

Tom moved his mount closer to Pollard's and positioned himself slightly behind the killer. He slipped his gun from its holster and reversed his grip on it. He was going to wallop Pollard with the gun butt hard enough to knock him out for a few minutes, then untie him, move his saddle to the extra horse, and lash him back into place on it before he regained consciousness.

That was the plan, anyway.

"You make me sick at my stomach," Pollard said. "You go on and on about the law but all you really want is revenge. You can't stand the thought of what I did to that gal—and I don't just mean slicing her face up."

"Keep talking," Tom said as his hand tightened around the Colt.

Maybe it would be all right to enjoy this a little after all.

He lifted his arm and brought it down, striking fast at the back of Pollard's head. Pollard ducked and twisted out of the way of the blow, then kept turning, something he shouldn't have been able to do.

As Pollard's arms flashed up, Tom saw, to his horror, that the prisoner's hands were free. He had no idea how Pollard had managed that and no time to ponder the question because both of Pollard's hands locked around Tom's wrist and dragged the deputy toward him.

The horses spooked again and started running. They would have shied apart but Pollard's hands were locked around Tom's wrist and Tom's legs were clamped around his mount, so that kept the horses together as the men atop them fought in desperate silence. Pollard jerked Tom's arm back and forth in an attempt to shake the gun free. Tom struck at Pollard with his other hand but the blows didn't land cleanly or with any real power.

With neither man able to control his mount, the horses veered into the trees. Tom rammed a shoulder into a low-hanging branch and the impact nearly knocked him out of the saddle. It was enough to jolt the Colt out of his fingers.

Seeing that the deputy had dropped the gun, Pollard let go of Tom's wrist and lunged at him. He got one hand on Tom's neck and used the other to sink a fist into his belly. Tom rammed the heel of his right hand under Pollard's chin and drove the prisoner's head back.

Then the horses reached the creek and splashed into it. Tom felt himself slipping from the saddle and fought to hang on but he couldn't manage it. At the last second, he kicked his feet out of the stirrups so the animal wouldn't drag him. He toppled into empty air.

Pollard still had him by the throat, though, and the fingers bore down with crushing force. As if the world wasn't spinning crazily enough, the lack of oxygen began to make Tom's head swim even more.

Pollard caught hold of Tom's shirtfront with his other hand and hauled him up. The man was incredibly strong—or else he fought with the strength of the madman he was. He lowered his head and butted Tom in the face. The blow was like an explosion that blasted Tom's wits from him completely.

He didn't actually lose consciousness but he was so stunned that, for several moments, he had no idea what was going on. When awareness returned to him, he realized that he was draped face-down over the back of Pollard's horse in front of the saddle. Pollard pawed through Tom's pockets until he found what he was looking for: the folding Barlow knife that Tom always carried.

With that in his grasp, Pollard hung on to Tom with his other hand, opened the blade with his teeth, and bent over to saw at the rope around his right ankle. Tom kept the knife sharp and it cut through the bonds in a matter of seconds.

Then Pollard gave Tom a shove that sent him sliding backward off the horse. The deputy landed in the creek and went under the water. He came up splashing and spluttering.

Tom hadn't gotten a chance to spit out all the water he had swallowed when Pollard's arm looped around his neck from behind and he felt the touch of steel against his throat.

"I'm gonna' enjoy this," Pollard whispered gleefully into Tom's ear.

15

BRADDOCK'S INSTINCTS SET OFF ALARM BELLS IN HIS
brain as he spotted the dark shape in the middle of the
trail up ahead. He hauled back on the buckskin's reins
and reached for the Winchester. As he slid the rifle out
of its saddle sheath, his head swiveled smoothly back
and forth. To his right was a creek with a number of
trees growing on its banks. To the left lay a stretch of
open ground about twenty yards wide with a rocky,
cactus-dotted slope rising on its other side.

Those trees could provide cover for a bushwhacker
and so could the boulders on top of the rise. Braddock
knew that if he continued along the trail, he could be
riding into a trap.

But that huddled shape lying in the trail vaguely
resembled a man, so he knew he couldn't just turn and
ride away.

He nudged the horse into a slow, wary walk,
guiding it with his knees while he held the Winchester
in both hands, ready for instant use. The rifle already
had a bullet in the chamber.

The thud of the buckskin's hooves against the hard-packed trail sounded loud in the night. The shape in the trail stirred slightly and a faint moan came from it, proving that it was human.

Braddock used his left hand to grasp the reins and bring the buckskin to a stop, then threw his right leg over the horse's back and slid from the saddle. He dropped lightly to the ground.

"Tom?" he asked quietly.

The man in the trail groaned again. Braddock walked toward him, turning a little from side to side to scan his surroundings. As far as he could tell, he and Tom Nation were the only people for miles around but Braddock didn't believe that for a second.

He dropped to a knee beside the huddled shape. Tom Nation lay curled up on his side. When Braddock put a hand on his shoulder, he gasped and flinched.

"It's all right, Tom," Braddock told him. "It's me, G.W. Braddock."

He eased the deputy over onto his back. Light from the moon and stars revealed that Tom's face was awash with blood from a number of cuts.

Braddock knew without being told that he was looking at Henry Pollard's work.

Anger stabbed deep into the Ranger. He had known he was taking a big chance by sending Tom to Fort Davis with Pollard but it had seemed like the only way to prevent a lynching without shedding a lot of innocent blood. It had worked out as Braddock planned but blood had been shed anyway—Tom Nation's blood.

Braddock lifted his head and looked around. He didn't see Tom's horse or any of the other horses. That meant Henry Pollard had four mounts now. He could ride hard and fast, switching back and forth, and be dozens of miles away by the end of the new day.

It didn't matter how far Pollard went, Braddock thought. He would track him down.

But first, he had to get some help for the injured deputy. He checked Tom's body and didn't find any stab wounds. Apparently, loss of blood and shock from the injuries to his face had been enough to leave the deputy half-senseless. Pollard hadn't tried to kill him.

Just mutilate him.

Holding the Winchester in his right hand, Braddock used his left to lift Tom into a sitting position, then got that arm around the deputy's slender frame. He straightened from his crouch and hauled Tom up with him.

"Come on," Braddock said. "I think we're closer to Fort Davis than Alpine, so we'll go on there."

He led Tom toward the buckskin, half-carrying him. They were almost there when the horse suddenly shied, warning Braddock. He let go of Tom, causing the deputy to slump to the ground again, and tried to swing the Winchester toward the hurtling shape that came around the buckskin.

The attacker bent low, got a shoulder under the rifle's barrel, and rammed it skyward as he crashed into Braddock. The man's weight drove the Ranger backward. He dropped the Winchester since it wasn't much good at close quarters like this and grappled with the shadowy figure as he tried to keep his balance.

Braddock lost that fight and went over backward. Henry Pollard landed on top of him and drove the air out of his lungs. Pollard dug a knee into Braddock's belly as well.

Braddock hadn't had the fight knocked out of him, though. He shot his right fist up and slammed it into Pollard's jaw. That rocked the man's head back. Braddock plastered his left hand over Pollard's face and tried to gouge his eyes out. Pollard roared in pain and fury and jerked his head away. Braddock arched his back and bucked Pollard to the side.

Braddock rolled the other way, came up on hands and knees gasping for breath. He barely had time to gulp down some air before Pollard tackled him again. The two men rolled across the trail, slugging brutally at each other.

The punches he took made red lights dance in front of Braddock's eyes but he gave as good as he got. Pollard tried to knee him in the groin but Braddock twisted out of the way. He slashed the edge of his right hand across Pollard's throat, making the killer gag. A second later, Braddock's left fist caught Pollard on the side of the head and stunned him.

Braddock knew better than to ease up. He rammed his right fist into Pollard's belly up to the wrist, then chopped another left to his face. He felt cartilage crunch as Pollard's nose flattened under that blow. Braddock drove two more hard, swift rights into Pollard's jaw, driving his head far to the side.

Pollard slumped back on the ground, unable to move.

Breathing hard, heart slugging in his chest, Braddock heaved himself off the senseless killer. He staggered to his feet and reached down to his side to see if his Colt was still in its holster. It was, so Braddock began to slide it out.

He hadn't cleared leather when he heard Tom Nation choke out a warning.

It came too late. Something exploded on the back of Braddock's head and sent him pitching forward into oblivion.

THE PAIN that seeped into Braddock's consciousness told him he was still alive but that was the only thing welcome about it. Slowly, he became aware that he was on his feet. His arms were raised at his sides and something was keeping them in that position. He didn't try to move because he didn't want Pollard and whoever had knocked him out to know just yet that he was awake. Instead, he opened his eyes the thinnest slit and listened for what was going on around him.

He couldn't see anything except what appeared to be part of the Fort Davis trail in front of him. He heard something, though: voices murmured somewhere not far off. Two men, from the sound of them, but he couldn't make out what they were saying.

Then the voices became clearer and Braddock knew the men were coming toward him. Henry Pollard told someone, "Get some water in your hat and throw it on Braddock. I'm tired of waiting for him to wake up."

"Sí, señor," the other man replied.

Because of that warning, Braddock expected the creek water that splashed in his face a few moments later. He acted like it took him by surprise anyway, sputtering and jerking his head from side to side.

"Welcome back to the land of the living, Braddock," Pollard said. He laughed. "For a little while, anyway."

Braddock opened his eyes all the way and looked around. He was strung up between two of the cottonwoods with pieces of rope binding his wrists to the trees. His arms were pulled out tight enough to make his shoulder sockets ache.

Tom Nation was in the same predicament, stretched between two of the other trees. The young man's head hung far forward. He was either dead or unconscious. From where he was, Braddock couldn't tell which.

Pollard's companion was a stocky, heavily beard-stubbled Mexican. To the best of Braddock's memory, he had never seen the man before. He could make a guess as to the Mexican's identity, though. The man had to be one of the few survivors from the gang of hired killers that had stormed the jail.

Pollard stood in front of Braddock with an expression of gloating satisfaction on his face. He went on, "You're probably wondering how I got loose, aren't you, Ranger?" He held up both hands with the sleeves of his shirt pushed back so that his wrists were revealed. Both of them were raw and bloody, with great hunks of skin torn off them. "It's amazing how much you can accomplish if you don't care how much it hurts. I twisted them back and forth until I'd worked some play into the ropes. An animal will chew its own leg off to get free from a trap, you know. I would have done the same if I'd had to. I tried to tell the deputy he'd never get me to Fort Davis."

"You're...crazy...Pollard," Braddock ground out.

"You say that but, from where I'm standing, *I'm* the sane one. It's the rest of the world that's crazy. And who's to say which one of us is right?"

The Mexican said, "It might be a good idea for you to go ahead and kill them, Señor Pollard. Dearborn may have wired the sheriff in Fort Davis to be expecting you and the deputy and he could send out somebody to look for you if you don't show up."

"We don't have to worry about that until later, Santiago," Pollard replied. "I intend to be gone by then. Although I must admit, the idea of making these two sons of bitches die as slowly as possible definitely appeals to me. I've heard it said that the Apaches can take up to eight hours having their sport with a prisoner before he finally dies. You think I could match that?"

"I think you'd be foolish to try," the man called Santiago said. "The rest of the Rangers are gonna' be after you, not to mention every other lawman in this part of the country. The smart thing for you to do is come to Mexico with me. I know places south of the border where no one will ever find you."

"Spend the rest of my life hiding out in your Godforsaken country?" Pollard snorted in derision at that idea. "I don't think so. When I get through with these two, I'm going to head for my brother's ranch. Amos will help me. He'll give me a place to hide out until the uproar dies down and I can go back to my old life. You'll see. Money and power can do everything."

"You're wrong about that," Braddock said. "After all the atrocities you've carried out, the law will never stop looking for you, Pollard. You'll be a fugitive the rest of your life until they catch up to you and put a noose around your neck."

Pollard's lips drew back from his teeth in a snarl as he put his face close to Braddock's.

"You'll never know whether you're right or not, Ranger," he said. "You'll be dead by then." He raised the knife he held and waved it back and forth slowly in front of Braddock's eyes. "Cutting you up isn't good enough. It was great fun doing that to the Castle girl, and to the deputy, too, but you deserve something even better. I'm going to start by peeling every bit of skin from your face. You'll feel it come tearing off, inch by inch, strip by strip—"

"Henry!" a new voice roared. "By God, that's enough!"

16

Pollard jerked around in surprise. He had been so caught up in tormenting his captive that he hadn't noticed anyone approaching.

Neither had Braddock. Santiago had, though. He bolted toward his horse and was halfway there when two more men loomed up and leveled guns at him.

"Hold it right there, hombre," one of the newcomers drawled. Santiago stopped short and stood there with his arms half-raised, keeping his hands well away from his gun and the knife sheathed on his other hip.

A tall, erect figure stalked toward Henry Pollard. Henry exclaimed, "Amos! How in the world did you find me?"

"Never mind that," Amos Pollard snapped. "Did I hear you threatening to torture this Ranger to death?"

"Well, of course I am," Henry replied as if his answer was the most obvious thing in the world. "What else would I do? He wants to take me in and hang me!"

"That's what a lawman does. He sees to it that a murderer gets what's coming to him."

"A murderer?" Henry repeated as he stared at his brother. "I'm no murderer. *I'm* the one who sees that people get what's coming to them. I'm the one who punishes anybody who crosses me and anybody who helps them."

"Like all those people you and your hired guns killed in Santa Angelina?"

"Exactly!" Henry said, grinning now. "I knew you'd understand, Amos. Those people took the Castle girl's side against me. You know how they must have talked, the things they're bound to have said. They thought I was terrible because I paid her back for cutting me the way she did, the little slut—"

Amos Pollard's arm flashed up in a savage backhanded blow that cracked across his brother's face and made Henry stagger to the side. He stared at Amos in disbelief and said, "But...but—"

Amos hit him again, this time with a closed fist. Henry reeled back. Amos went after him, sledging blow after blow to his face and body. Henry fell to his knees and Amos hit him one last time, stretching him out senseless on the ground.

Breathing heavily, Amos turned to the two men he had brought with him. He said, "Bert, you keep that Mexican covered. Ray, cut these two men loose."

"Sure, boss," the burly cowhand called Ray replied. He pouched the iron he'd been holding, took a knife from his belt, and hurried over to Braddock.

The Ranger inclined his head toward Tom Nation and said, "I'm all right. Tend to the deputy first."

Ray nodded and went to Tom's side.

"Is he alive?" Braddock asked.

"He's breathin'," Ray replied as he started sawing at the rope holding Tom's right arm to the tree trunk. "Pretty bloody, but he's alive."

It didn't take long to get Tom loose. Ray lowered him gently to the ground, then turned to Braddock. A few moments later the Ranger was free as well, muscles throbbing in pain as he was able to lower his stretched-out arms at last. He rubbed each of his shoulders in turn as he asked, "What now, Pollard?"

Amos Pollard gave him a cold, level stare and said, "What do you mean?"

"You've got your brother back," Braddock said. "What are you going to do with him?"

"Shouldn't you be asking what I'm going to do with *you?* You're the one who's been trying to make sure Henry keeps his date with the hangman."

"It's my job," Braddock said as he shrugged. At this moment, the knowledge that he had been stripped of his badge and bringing criminals to justice *wasn't* his job didn't even enter his thoughts. In his mind, right now, he *was* a Texas Ranger even if the star-in-a-circle emblem pinned to his shirt had a bullet hole in the center of it.

Amos Pollard didn't answer the question Braddock had asked him. Instead, he turned to the man who had cut the prisoners loose and said, "Ray, get my brother on his feet. I need to talk to him. Braddock, if you want to tend to Deputy Nation, that's fine. I don't bear any ill will toward either of you."

Braddock could have made some sort of sharp reply to that but he was more concerned with Tom Nation's condition at the moment. He went to the deputy's side, knelt, and lifted him into a sitting position. Tom stirred a little and muttered something as he tried to struggle back to consciousness.

The front of his shirt was dark with the blood that had welled from the wounds on his face but Braddock thought he would be all right if he had some medical attention. Those cuts needed to be cleaned and bandaged. It was difficult to tell in the light of the lowering moon but Braddock thought the injuries weren't as numerous or as deep as the ones that had disfigured June Castle. Henry must have hurried his butchery. Tom would carry some scars but not to the same extent as June.

Ray hauled Henry Pollard to his feet and stood him in front of Amos, holding him up so he wouldn't collapse again. Amos caught hold of his brother's chin and lifted his head.

"Henry, listen to me," Amos said. "Can you hear me?"

"Yeah, I...I guess," Henry slurred. "Why'd you...hit me, Amos?"

"What am I going to do with you, Henry?"

Before answering, Henry lifted a shaking hand and used the back of it to wipe away blood that had leaked from his mouth where his brother had hit him. He said, "Wha...what do you mean? You need to kill those two lawmen. They want to hang me!"

"I'm not a killer," Amos said.

Henry was getting some of his strength back. He shook loose of Ray's hand and said, "Gimme' a gun, then. I'll take care of 'em."

"I thought you wanted to use a knife on them. That's what you said, wasn't it? You were boasting about how much suffering you were going to inflict on them. I heard you with my own ears."

"Oh, for God's sake!" Henry burst out. "Don't tell me you're feelin' sorry for a couple of damn lawdogs! If you don't want to kill them, then don't. Let's just get out of here. I'm ready to go home." He looked around and added, "You can tell Luttrell to stop pointing that gun at Quintero, too. He's with me."

"Yes, I know he is," Amos said. "You think you can just go home after everything you've done, Henry?"

"Why the hell not? Nobody can prove I did anything except teach June Castle a lesson. Everybody kept going on about how I was responsible for what happened in Santa Angelina. There's no proof of that, not one damned bit! Quintero's not gonna testify that I paid him and the others to raid that worthless little settlement. So let's go back to the ranch and you can pay that trollop enough to shut her up for good and I can get on with my life, damn it!"

Tom Nation's senses must have returned enough for him to understand what Henry was saying. He yelled, "Shut up! You...you can't talk that way about June!"

He tried to stand up but his strength deserted him. He sagged against Braddock.

Henry turned to look at the deputy and laughed. He said, "I forget for a minute how sweet you are on her, Tom! Maybe you can court her now, after all, since the two of you match. Hell, you ought to be thanking me!"

"Henry." Amos Pollard's voice was flat and hard. "You think you can just come back to the ranch and go on being the way you've always been? Hurting anybody you want just because the fancy strikes you?"

Henry grunted and said, "Why not? My brother's the richest, most important man in the county."

Amos stared at him for a long moment and then the rancher's shoulders slumped. Braddock had never seen a man look so defeated. Quietly, Amos said, "You've got a rope on your saddle, don't you, Ray?"

"Sure, boss," Ray replied. "A cowboy never goes anywhere without a rope."

"Can you make a hangman's knot?"

Ray didn't answer the question. In the stunned silence that followed it, Henry made a choked noise and then said, "Amos, what are you talking about?"

"I would have gone to any lengths to save you," Amos said. "Now I see that I can't."

Henry stared at him for several heartbeats, then abruptly threw back his head and laughed.

"Son of a bitch! For a second there you had me believin' you, big brother. That's a pretty good one. If you're tryin' to scare me into behaving myself, well, it worked. Whew!"

"I'm not trying to scare you. I just see now that you're never going to change. You really are like the mad dog that everyone compares you to. You're a threat to everybody around you."

Henry's face twisted in a hate-filled grimace. He said, "Well, aren't you the high and mighty one? Can't you hear yourself, Amos? You're spoutin' words like a damned preacher! You want me to change? Why should I? I'm better than everybody else! Other people, they're just fucking cattle, just like the stock on the ranch. If I want to slaughter 'em, I've got every right to."

Amos Pollard backed off a step and drew his gun as he told Ray, "Get your rope and make a noose. Then bring it and your horse over here."

"Amos," Ray said softly, "are you sure—"

"Just do what I ask you, Ray. We've been friends a long time. Just do it."

Ray sighed and turned toward his horse.

From where he still knelt beside Tom, supporting the injured deputy, Braddock said, "You're taking the law into your own hands, Pollard. That makes you a criminal, too."

"No, what made me a criminal was protecting my brother and turning a blind eye to his perversions all these years," Amos said with a shake of his head. "I'm just trying to put a stop to that the best way I know how."

"Then let's all go into Fort Davis, lock him up, and wait for the judge. That's the right way to do it."

"That might be the legal way," Amos Pollard said, "but it's not the *right* way. The right way is to end it here and now. It's my responsibility. Maybe you've always followed the law, Ranger, but sometimes you have to step outside of it."

Those words pierced Braddock and with them came the memory of how *he* had stepped outside the law. He had pinned on a badge he had no right to, had led people to believe he was still a Ranger when he really wasn't.

He was an outlaw, too.

"You're crazy!" Henry yelled. "You're all crazy! Amos, you're my brother. You can't hang me!"

"I can put down a mad dog," Amos grated. "Ray, you have that noose ready?"

"Just about," Ray replied. "I ain't sure about this, though. Seems like the Ranger's right, Amos. This ain't the way to handle it."

"Do you want to go on pulling Henry's fat out of

the fire? Do you want to have a hand in the death of whoever he kills next?"

"Well, I reckon when you put it like that..."

Ray finished fashioning the noose and led the horse over under the trees where the others were standing. Henry was getting jittery now, Braddock thought as he watched the young man. He looked like he wanted to make a break of some sort but the gun held rock-steady in his brother's hand stopped him.

"That branch will do," Amos said, using his free hand to point. "Throw the rope over it."

Ray sighed and followed the order. He tossed the noose end of the rope over the cottonwood branch and tied the other end to the trunk.

"I won't do it," Henry declared. "Damn you, Amos, I won't do it."

"Then I'll just shoot you, same as I would a mad dog."

For a tense few seconds, it looked like that was what was going to happen. Then, unexpectedly, Henry laughed again.

"You're still just trying to scare me," he said. "You think if you make me climb up there and put that noose around my neck, I'll be so scared I'll shit my pants and promise to be good. Well, you *don't* scare me, big brother, and I'll prove it." He stuck a foot in the stirrup, grabbed the saddle horn, and swung up onto the horse's back. He took hold of the noose and slipped it over his head. "There! I'm ready to hang! Are you done making a fool of yourself yet, Amos?"

Tipping his head back slightly, Amos Pollard looked up at his younger brother. As Braddock watched the drama unfold, he realized he could see

263

them more clearly now. The eastern sky was gray with light. Dawn wasn't far off.

And as Braddock looked at Amos Pollard, he saw the emotions warring on the rancher's hawk-like face. He could imagine what was going through Amos's thoughts. His mind had to be filled with memories, maybe of Henry's boyhood, of a time before he'd been a killer, when he still had a shred of innocence and hope and promise to him...

Braddock knew what it was like to be haunted by the past and, in that moment, he had no idea whether Amos Pollard was going to go through with this or not.

Then, a grotesque gurgling sound broke the silence and Braddock jerked his head around to see the other Triangle P cowboy collapsing with blood pouring from his throat. The hired killer called Quintero was beside him, the knife he had just used to cut Bert's throat clutched in his left hand. Braddock figured Bert had taken his attention off the prisoner to watch the dramatic tableau under the trees, just long enough to be fatal.

Quintero's right hand was full of the gun he had jerked from its holster and flame spurted from its muzzle as he hammered shots at Amos Pollard.

AMOS STAGGERED AS HE WAS HIT AT LEAST ONCE. RAY let out a furious yell and leaped toward him but before he could reach his employer and long-time friend, one of Quintero's slugs ripped through him, too, and spun him off his feet. The gun he was holding flew from his hand.

And landed next to Braddock.

The outlaw Ranger scooped up the weapon and fired from where he knelt beside Tom Nation. Instinct and a sure hand guided the three shots he squeezed off. All three bullets pounded into Santiago Quintero's chest, knocking him back a couple of steps in a macabre, jittering dance. Quintero dropped his gun, pawed at the holes in his chest, then spun around and collapsed.

Amos Pollard, Ray, and Bert were all down but, before he could check on them, Braddock sprang up and dashed over to Quintero to kick the revolver out of the man's reach. He was pretty sure Quintero was in no shape to use the gun again but taking chances could cost a man his life.

He put the toe of his boot under Quintero's shoulder and rolled the killer onto his back. Quintero gasped and spasmed. He said, "I thought...I thought if I helped him...Henry would...reward me..."

He straightened out and sighed as he died.

Braddock swung around. In the flurry of gunfire, he had lost track of Henry Pollard but he saw now that the shots had caused Ray's horse to bolt out from under him. Henry swung from the noose, kicking feebly. Braddock walked over and looked up at him.

Henry must have tried to get his fingers under the rope in time to keep it from tightening on his neck but he'd been too slow. The noose had jerked closed when his weight hit it and dug into his flesh so deeply that he couldn't pry it out. His face was dark red, almost purple, and his eyes bugged out so far it looked like they were about to come out of their sockets.

He made some noises, and after a moment Braddock realized they were words. Henry was pleading for his life, saying, "Help...me...help...you're...a Ranger..."

Braddock drew in a deep breath and shook his head.

"No," he said. "Not really."

Then he turned his back on Henry Pollard and went to check on the other men. By the time he discovered that Ray and Bert were both dead but Amos Pollard was still alive, Henry had stopped kicking and hung still and silent instead.

THE SUN WAS WELL up when Braddock and Tom Nation reined in their horses on a rise overlooking the town of Fort Davis. What was left of the abandoned military post that gave the settlement its name was visible just north of town.

The light of day had confirmed what Braddock thought about Tom's injuries. They would heal and, although they would leave scars, he would be all right. Physically, anyway. No one could predict how wounds of the other sort would mend.

Behind them, linked together with a lead rope, were the horses Braddock had found hidden in the trees along the creek, where Henry Pollard had hidden, too, before crawling out to jump Braddock because he didn't have a gun to ambush him. The horses carried the bodies of Henry Pollard, Raymond Harper, Bert Luttrell, and Santiago Quintero.

Amos Pollard was back there, too, riding hunched over in the saddle, a crude bandage around his bullet-shattered shoulder. He hadn't said a word since Braddock had lifted him onto the horse. He'd looked over at his brother's body, roped face-down over one of the other animals, and silence had been his only response.

That, and a look in his eyes as if grief had begun to consume him from the inside out, a slow, agonizing process that would end only in death.

"I'm sorry I let you down, Ranger," Tom said as he and Braddock sat on their horses. "I didn't get Henry here so the law could deal with him."

"Sometimes the law has to take what it can get," Braddock said.

Tom hesitated, then went on, "What did you mean...when you told Henry you aren't really a Ranger? You've got a badge..."

"With a bullet hole in it."

"That doesn't make a difference. It's still a Ranger badge."

"It's too long a story to tell," Braddock said. "You can make it on into town from here. I have other places I need to be."

Back across the border, he thought. Back in Esperanza, where he wasn't an outlaw, only a man without a home.

Braddock started to turn the buckskin away, then paused and added, "Henry Pollard said one thing worth listening to. June Castle's going to need a friend. I reckon you're better qualified for that job than anybody else."

"Because I'm carved up and ugly, too?" Tom asked, unable to keep the bitterness out of his voice.

"Because you care for her," Braddock said. "And ugly's just like beauty...all in the eye of the beholder."

He lifted a hand in farewell and headed south, back to Mexico, and, as he rode, he wondered if he would ever be back.

He supposed that would depend on whether Texas had need of an outlaw Ranger.

TAKE A LOOK AT VOLUME TWO

BY JAMES REASONER

New York Times **bestselling author James Reasoner returns to the Old West in this gritty, compelling action-packed saga!**

A savage ambush – twenty men slaughtered in a brutal massacre and a fortune in gold stolen – was a crime big enough and bold enough to bring the Outlaw Ranger to the wide-open settlement of Cemetery Butte. No atrocity prepared G.W. Braddock for the evil that awaited him, stretching bloody hands out of the past.

From one showdown to the next, Braddock finds himself with an unexpected ally: an ancient Indian who claims to be the last war chief of the Comanche. This time around, their pursuit will lead them to a bloody showdown on the Texas plains, with the lives of innocents hanging in the balance!

Outlaw Ranger, Volume 2 includes: Blood and Gold and The Last War Chief.

COMING OCTOBER 2021

ABOUT THE AUTHOR

James Reasoner has been telling tales and spinning yarns as far back as he can remember. He's been doing it professionally for more than 40 years, and during that time, under his own name and dozens of pseudonyms, he's written almost 400 novels and more than 100 shorter pieces of fiction. His books have appeared on the *New York Times, USA Today,* and *Publishers Weekly* bestseller lists. He has written Westerns, mysteries, historical sagas, war novels, science fiction and fantasy, and horror fiction.

Growing up in the late Fifties and early Sixties when every other series on television was a Western made him into a lifelong fan of the genre. The Lone Ranger, Roy Rogers, Hopalong Cassidy, Matt Dillon, and John Wayne made quite an impression on him. At the age of 10, he discovered Western novels when he checked out *Single Jack* by Max Brand and *Hopalong Cassidy* (there's that name again!) by Clarence E. Mulford from the library bookmobile that came out every Saturday to the small town in Texas where he lived. He's been reading Westerns ever since, long before he started writing them, and always will.

James Reasoner has also written numerous articles, essays, and book introductions on a variety of topics related to popular culture, including vintage paperbacks and the publishing industry, pulp magazines, comics, movies, and TV. He writes the popular blog *Rough Edges* and is the founder and moderator of an email group devoted to Western pulp magazines.

He lives in the same small town in Texas where he grew up and is married to the popular mystery novelist Livia J. Washburn, who has also written Westerns under the name L.J. Washburn.

Printed in Great Britain
by Amazon

80278169R00161